STRANGERS IN TOWN

They had been in there about twenty minutes when two breath-taking strangers came in. It had to be a breath-taking arrival to halt a debate in the Dog.

These two were tarts. Not Upper Crudshaw tarts. Not tarts of a calibre that one could ever picture operating in Upper Crudshaw; tarts who would have drawn attention to their tartiness even in the most sinful corners of Bradburn. They were almost but not quite punk-cult figures: hair in a spiky tightness that drew attention to the barely credible smallness of their skulls. But their hair was not dyed in unmentionable colours: one was raven-black, the other had the makings of a Nashville Goldilocks. One was in black leather, including a mini-skirt that looked as if it would split if she attempted a pace of more than nine inches. The other wore a flared trouser-suit with a collar that hung to where her belly-button was and had had a distant origin in naval rig. Both were made up with their eyes beaded down in deep black sockets. Both looked as if their faces would crack like the glaze of over-heated porcelain if they were to risk a smile.

The newcomers asked for Bacardi *and* rum. With his Dalesman's urbanity, the landlord served them without comment. Then one of them asked if he could direct them to the vicarage.

Bantam offers the finest in classic and modern British murder mysteries. Ask your bookseller for the books you have missed.

Agatha Christie
Death on the Nile
A Holiday for Murder
The Mousetrap and Other Plays
The Mysterious Affair at Styles
Poirot Investigates
Postern of Fate
The Secret Adversary
The Seven Dials Mystery
Sleeping Murder

Margery Allingham
Black Plumes
Death of a Ghost
The Fashion in Shrouds

Dorothy Simpson
Last Seen Alive
The Night She Died
Puppet for a Corpse
Six Feet Under
Close Her Eyes

Sheila Radley
The Chief Inspector's Daughter
Death in the Morning
Fate Worse Than Death
Coming Soon: Who Saw Him Die?

Elizabeth George
A Great Deliverance

Colin Dexter
The Riddle of the Third Mile
The Lost World of Nicholas Quinn
Service of All the Dead
The Dead of Jericho
Coming Soon: The Secret of
   Annexe 3

John Greenwood
The Mind of Mr. Mosley
The Missing Mr. Mosley
Mosley by Moonlight
Murder, Mr. Mosley
Mists Over Mosley

Ruth Rendell
The Face of Trespass
The Lake of Darkness
No More Dying Then
One Across, Two Down
Shake Hands Forever
A Sleeping Life
A Dark-Adapted Eye
   (writing as Barbara Vine)
A Fatal Inversion
   (writing as Barbara Vine)

Marian Babson
Death in Fashion
Reel Murder
Coming Soon: Murder, Murder
   Little Star

Christianna Brand
Suddenly at His Residence
Heads You Lose

Dorothy Cannell
The Widows Club

THE MIND OF
MR. MOSLEY

John Greenwood

BANTAM BOOKS
TORONTO · NEW YORK · LONDON · SYDNEY · AUCKLAND

All characters and events portrayed in this story are
fictitious.

This edition contains the complete text
of the original hardcover edition.
NOT ONE WORD HAS BEEN OMITTED.

THE MIND OF MR. MOSLEY
A Bantam Book / published by arrangement with
Walker Publishing Company, Inc.

PRINTING HISTORY
Walker edition published January 1987
Bantam edition / August 1988

ISBN 0-553-27120-2

Bantam Books are published by Bantam Books, a division of Bantam
Doubleday Dell Publishing Group, Inc. Its trademark, consisting of
the words "Bantam Books" and the portrayal of a rooster, is Reg-
istered in U.S. Patent and Trademark Office and in other countries.
Marca Registrada. Bantam Books, 666 Fifth Avenue, New York, New
York 10103

PRINTED IN THE UNITED STATES OF AMERICA

KR   0 9 8 7 6 5 4 3 2 1

THE MIND OF
MR. MOSLEY

Chapter One

"This is one of yours, I think, Mosley."

The Assistant Chief Constable had just caught a whiff from Mosley's pipe, which had enabled him to deduce that the most wayward of his inspectors had condescended to drop in at the office this morning. Mosley had in fact come for a packet of paper-clips.

The Assistant Chief Constable had just embarked upon that most melancholy first chore in his daily discipline, the overnight *Sudden Death* file. He found it a melancholy duty because, as he had just said to Detective-Superintendent Tom Grimshaw, who was looking over his shoulder, it was becoming increasingly common for him to meet more or less warmly cherished acquaintances in that manilla folder. Grimshaw was waiting to see if any items in this morning's accumulation would be coming his way. They very seldom did. Usually the crop of unexpected departures were men of the ACC'S age-group whose cardio-vascular system had thrown in the towel after excesses at the meal-table or in some over-demanding extra-marital bed. There were other, though rarer, predisposing causes on record: excitement whilst responding to an after-dinner toast, even the imminence of an annual audit. But the wilful despatch of one's neighbours was infrequent in Bradburn. Bradburn men, when they departed this life without preliminary notice, almost invariably did so as the outcome of routine wear, tear and abuse.

"Upper Crudshaw: I believe that's one of the localities that you own, Mosley."

Mosley came into the inner office, held his hand out for the file, read it over—and did not react quite as the ACC expected him to. True, this was not a commonplace case of coronary occlusion. It was one of those suicides from which even the laconic oral comments of the GP who had examined the cadaver on the spot had banished any possibility of foul play. Mosley ought, according to the form-

1

book, to have said something formal, philosophical and final. Such as, "Oh, aye, well—"

But he didn't. He stared at the file as if there was something in it that he did not quite understand. Then, having finally compelled himself to grasp it, he looked as if he did not believe what he had grasped. The ACC and Tom Grimshaw both knew the symptoms and saw them without joy. They signified that Mosley was on to something—something that he would keep to himself, perhaps for obdurate months, until he was as sure as only Mosley could be sure.

"A friend of yours, Mosley?"

"I knew him."

"It looks straightforward enough to me."

There was no doubt that it was suicide. Reuben Tunnicliffe, a man in his seventies, had hanged himself by his braces from a deeply driven-in nail in his outside earth-closet. There were no marks on the body to suggest that any second party had assisted in any way, by invitation or otherwise.

"But of course, if there's anything you're unhappy about, Mosley, you'd better take a discreet look. It's quite a time since you were in Upper Crudshaw."

"Last Thursday."

"You didn't put anything in writing about it," Tom Grimshaw said without emphasis, and too wearily to convey animus. If Mosley had put pen to paper about a routine visit, it would have meant that he was covering his flanks in preparation for something even more than usually devious, something that could only herald trouble in the remote future. Mosley appeared to be hovering in front of the ACC's desk. Normally he was indecently anxious to get away.

"Was there anything else, Mosley?"

"I came in for some paper-clips, but I don't seem to be able to find any requisition forms."

The ACC put a handful of clips from his own desk-tidy into an envelope and handed it to Mosley with a gesture of broad magnanimity.

"We pride ourselves, Mosley, that our men on the ground are as well equipped for emergencies as any force in the kingdom."

Chapter Two

In some of the guide-books Upper Crudshaw is called a large village. In others, particularly the older ones, it is chartered as a small town. This is the status which the people of Crudshaw would have demanded, had anyone in the place seen any point in reading a guide-book about themselves. Upper Crudshaw is so far from anywhere else that it has always had to be self-supporting, and this is especially true in view of Crudshaw winters. When the youthful and sporting-minded in the soft southern under-belly of the kingdom are eagerly watching for the first filigree snowflakes to settle, Upper Crudshaw is usually well into its annual siege, with drifts reaching the height of bedroom windowsills and the warm breath from ewes' nostrils melting the holes in the snow that are their only hope against asphyxiation.

Upper Crudshaw therefore has one each of all the plainer types of shop, its own doctor and policeman, a post office and three public houses. Upper Crudshaw has always relied on its own resources, as the substantial remains of a medieval whipping-post demonstrate. In the inexorable march of progress it has lost its static fishmonger, who has now gone peripatetic, and its dental surgeon, who until the Second World War used to operate once a week in Hetty Wilson's back room with such instruments as he could carry in a small attaché case. It has a church, two chapels and a pharmacy, and the gritstone blocks of its largely eighteenth- and nineteenth-century cottages cling together at a fascinating conglomerate of irregular angles to reinforce each other against the climate.

Mosley went to see Dr. Artingstall, Reuben Tunnicliffe's GP, and established that apart from a bottle of expectorant last January—which Reuben, scorning antibiotics, had demanded by its trade name—he had neither sought nor needed medical attention for years.

"He did just say, in a roguish sort of way, that he didn't

3

seem to be able to manage quite as much of what he called
the other as he used to, and it was a pity you couldn't get
oysters on the National Health. I called him a dirty old
bugger and he went off laughing."

Reuben Tunnicliffe, who took his life at the age of 74,
had been a retired baker's journeyman, getting up at four
o'clock every morning throughout his working days to knead
dough at Hardcastles' in Union Street, and finishing punc-
tually on the day before his sixty-fifth birthday. But he had
been called in as recently as eighteen months ago when a
flu epidemic knocked half the staff out. He was also in great
demand among the undiscerning, whenever something special was wanted in the cake line. When Reuben Tunnicliffe
got an icing-bag in his hand, he was capable of soaring flights
of fancy in the realms of solid geometry and produced great
slabs of standard sentimentality that seemed to suit a broad
stratum of Crudshaw society. Reuben and Annie Tunnicliffe
had been married fifty-five years. They had been childhood
sweethearts; neither had ever as much as walked out with
anyone else. Annie was six years Reuben's senior, and that
introduced an interesting consideration. It meant that she
had been twenty when he, at fourteen, was still in the top
class at school. They had married when he was nineteen—
and she had been carrying their eldest for two months.
There was some speculation as to who had made the running. Had Annie been Reuben's willing teacher, having
spotted some aspect of his early puberty that had been
lacking in young men of her own age and intimate ac-
quaintance?

They had gone on to rear six children, including an af-
terthought conceived when Annie was in her forties. And
the six were now scattered about the hemispheres: an engineer on an astronomic Arab payroll in the Gulf, a girl
teaching musical composition and counterpoint at a Manchester college, another married to an egg-head in a silicon
valley. The youngest boy had wed a tribal chieftain's daughter and was lecturing on differential geometry at a university
in what used to be called the Belgian Congo. The only
member of the family who reappeared in Upper Crudshaw
with any regularity was Susan: the one with *cap and gown*

for music—Crudshaw always attached due weight to the outward trappings of distinction.

Mosley went to the funeral, sat in a pew far back, and afterwards observed the committal from an inconspicuous corner of the churchyard. Upper Crudshaw was paying its respects in force. But Mosley duly noted that the dead man's family was not represented. This would certainly be filed away for appropriate future reference by the local social arbiters: though there were in all fairness good enough reasons for it. Annie Tunnicliffe belonged to a generation that remembered the time when it was not considered a woman's place to go to funerals. And perhaps she was in no physical or emotional state to parade her grief in public.

The Tunnicliffes had been more than close—they had been inseparable. Whatever they had done, they had done together. Once a month they went on the bus to Bradburn market, and looked critically round the stalls together. Once a week, on Saturday nights, they went together to the Stonewrights' Arms, and Annie drank a milk stout while Reuben sipped his way through two pints of mild. Two or three times a year they went together on the Good Companions' coach to Whitby or Morecambe or the Abbeys, sitting together with Annie in the windowseat, quietly drawing each other's attention to such wonders as a bull in a field, a healthy row of shallots in an allotment garden or a flock of Christmas dinners fattening.

Up to a few years ago they had never missed their annual week's holiday, and they had always gone to Southport. It was the death of their boarding house landlady that put an end to that. Neither of them was prepared to risk a possibly disastrous experiment.

"You'd have thought that daughter of theirs would have spared half a day to come and drop a handful of muck on her father's box."

"Oh, she's in Crudshaw. Haven't you seen the car she's got? Shouldn't be allowed on the road. Keeping her mother company for the afternoon, I suppose."

Annie Tunnicliffe and her daughter had not even risen to providing funeral meats: not as much as a ham sandwich to say nothing of the *de rigueur* buffet at the Stonewrights' or an outside caterer in the church hall. Upper Crudshaw made no comment, but again they stored their feelings for the day it might be fitting to remember them.

Mosley stayed long enough in the churchyard to read the labels on the wreaths and sprays, and then he made his way to the Tunnicliffes' home. This was a characteristic Crudshaw property in a lane behind the church: square-cut and solid—a house with its chin tucked in against the elements. It had always been kept in good condition, but with aggressive lack of finesse. Reuben had been too proud and active a man ever to allow anything to remain in visible disrepair. But as a general rule he would have done the house better service by leaving it alone. In everything he put his hands to, his craftsmanship lacked finish. He had never seen the necessity, for example, of masking a window-pane when painting the frame. The concrete surrounds with which he had embellished a drainage grid bore some resemblance to his work on the confectionary table. It was true that Reuben had flights of inventive fancy, but they were limited by the insensitivity of his fingers. No one but the faithful of Upper Crudshaw would have enthused about his cake icing, and then it was only those who were too mean-spirited to lay out hard-earned money on out-of-town expertise.

Susan Tunnicliffe came to the door: the Tunnicliffes' youngest, not far from the upper end of her thirties, smoking a cigarette and not wearing her *D. Mus.* gown and hood today, but a loose and long sweater in dog-turd brown and purple Levi cords. Mosley, like everybody else, had from time to time heard uncharitable rumours about Susan Tunnicliffe—enough for him to have consulted a former colleague who had moved on to Tameside for promotion to detective-sergeant. In her chosen field she was apparently regarded as one of the upper few, but she had never been one to allow a delicate specialism to deprive her of her earthier needs. At the moment, towards the fag-end of her nubile years, she was shacked up in Levenshulme with an unemployed Irishman who sometimes worked on building sites. And there had been earlier, equally macho, though perhaps superficially lovelier connections, but nothing that had ever even begun to look as if it was likely to last.

Susan did not know who Mosley was. He told her.

"I suppose you couldn't think of a better time to call? I thought we'd seen the last of you and your friends at the inquest."

"I just wanted to pay my respects to your mother. I was rather fond of your dad."

"Oh, aye?"

Susan Tunnicliffe had been born and bred in Upper Crudshaw. Alongside her improbable flair for baroque fugue went a scepticism nourished on millstone grit and the weatherswept moorlands. She was the sort of woman who did not actually *believe* in anything.

"I suppose you'd better come in. Mother—we have company. A scuffer."

Annie Tunnicliffe looked at Mosley without recognition, without pleasure and indeed without concern. Knocked sideways, Mosley told himself, doesn't know what to do with herself, probably never will be able to get herself straight again.

"I was always very fond of your husband," he said, repeating the formula, though he knew that Susan was looking at him with cynical contempt.

He began to take in the room. It was about what he had expected, give or take an ingredient or two. The radio was post-war—just. They had no television: Reuben had made excuses for not having one ever since they had been on the market. First he had said they would wait until colour sets came out. When that happened he was not prepared to lay out and buy one, and he would not rent one, because he believed that that was hire purchase, to which he had been implacably opposed all his life. The truth was that a lifetime of self-discipline had left both the Tunnicliffes unwilling to spend money, even though they were said not to be without.

"A mean old bugger," Mosley had heard someone call Reuben in a pub, an unfair comment within the ethos of Crudshaw, where it was imprinted in every man's genes to maintain a sinking-fund and never to let a soul know how much was in it.

"I wouldn't call him mean," somebody else had said.

"Bloody careful, though. Never even spent a penny of his army gratuity. He's had that making interest for forty years."

So they had this immediate post-war (secondhand) all-mains radio, and had bought nothing new in the way of furniture since the children, the eldest of whom was now in his fifties, had clambered over chairs and cushions. Otherwise there was a history of working-class culture in biscuit-tins and tea-caddies, a plaster head of Churchill and a clock exchanged for coupons from packet soup in the thirties. All clean: threadbare and untidy, because there were too many of the smaller props of living—little fish-paste jars stuffed with stubs of pencils, spills and last year's Haig poppies. There was an ancient office spike, loaded with receipted bills—they must go back decades. But there was no dust. The clipping hearth-rug was almost through to the hessian. The grate, which many a museum curator would have liked to see in one of his set-pieces, was black-leaded daily. Mosley thought that that had probably been one of Reuben's early morning chores; but the ritual had not been neglected, even in these last few disorganized days.

Useless to ask whether Reuben had shown any recent signs of depression. That had been put to several witnesses by the coroner, and each had hesitated, with an expression compounded of surprise and sheer blankness. Reuben would not of course have shown signs of gloom, however deeply he was oppressed. Upper Crudshaw was as jealous of its emotions as it was of its small savings. They were personal property. One did not admit to possessing them. If Reuben had been feeling down, he would have gone about striving to be more affable than ever, so that people would not know.

"Make Mr. Mosley a cup of tea."

So Annie Tunnicliffe did know him—knew at any rate who he was, though she had never had anything directly to do with him, nor he with her. When Mosley spoke of knowing people, it generally meant that he knew their names, their homes, something of the quality of their life, where they fitted into the kin-pattern of the district. He had seen the Tunnicliffes about together often enough over the years to have docketed away in his mind any odd thing that he had heard people say about them.

Annie Tunnicliffe was a little woman, hair white and thinning. It was difficult to look at her and think of her as the mother of six people now well on into life. It was even more difficult to think of her as a physical partner for Reuben, who was something of an ox of a man. She did not talk much, was probably out of tune with any style of dialogue other than her sixty-year-long conversation with her spouse. They would have had their own catch-phrases, their own esoteric vocabulary. It was extraordinarily difficult to find anthing to say to her now.

"These things happen, Mrs. Tunnicliffe. That's all I can say. I'm very, very sorry."

"*These things happen—*"

That was Susan Tunnicliffe. She had uncrossed her legs, but that was as far as she had got towards going to make the tea.

"*These things happen.* Now there speaks the voice of considered experience. You are a great comfort to us, Mr. Mosley."

"Get on with you," her mother said. "Go and mash tea."

Susan got up and went into the back kitchen.

"Very close, were Susan and her father," Mrs. Tunnicliffe said. "Doesn't know what to make of it. And nor don't I. What did the daft bugger want to go and do a thing like that for?"

That gave him the measure of her, Mosley thought. She was one of those women with an inner strength—something not to be mistaken for insensitivity—something that made her impervious to the batterings of circumstance. Of course, she would have sentimental setbacks. The next time she went on a coach-trip—if she ever did go on another coach-trip—she would turn her head to show Reuben an allotment row of onions and be hurtfully reminded that Reuben was not there. But it would take a deal more than that to make Annie Tunnicliffe go under. Annie Tunnicliffe would go on—not because she was telling herself she had to go on —but because she had been put on this earth to go on.

Mosley drank tea, and Susan must have had a crisis in that part of her conscience concerned with hospitality, because she also produced biscuits; or perhaps she wanted a biscuit herself. Mosley talked in clichés and platitudes that had the younger woman gaping at him in pity—though actually he was tailoring his speech with intuitive skill to what old Annie expected and would accept.

Nevertheless, it was a mercy to have an excuse to leave earlier than he otherwise might have done—because the Tunnicliffes had another visitor. It was Percy Darwent, another of Annie's generation, though younger than her—a mixture of the breezy and the arthritic, helped along with a stick.

"Nah, Annie. I've just come from t' churchyard. It went very well. Very well. A full turn-out. Upper Crudshaw did Reuben proud. You did as well to stay home, though. There was a fair draught whistling round them old yews."

He knew Mosley—everybody knew Mosley—though Mosley had not even heard of him before.

"Nah, Mr. Mosley. Come t' keep us in order, have you? Not taking Annie in this time, then?"

He laughed heartily. No one else did.

Susan Tunnicliffe saw Mosley out through the front door.

"Well—if there is anything—you know—if there's anything I can ever do—just get in touch," Mosley said.

"That's very kind of you, Mr. Mosley. But what had you in mind? What do you think might possibly crop up?"

She looked at him with excoriating hostility. He looked back at her, assessing. Was there in her eyes any evidence that she lived on an aesthetic plane apart from other worldlings? Could anyone guess from her appearance that she was a woman of uncommon and exacting talents? Or that she had cohabited with a series of men from distinctly lower slopes, presumably for no other satisfaction than what they produced from their loins—and the verve with which they produced it?

"One never knows, Miss Tunnicliffe."

"Ms."

Mosley ignored the correction.

"In fact, Mr. Mosley, not to put too fine a point on things—I can't imagine why you bothered to come."

Mosley walked down to the nuclear centre of Upper Crudshaw, a cobbled market place about the whipping-post. It would have made an excellent subject for a picture postcard if it had not also been a car park. Crudshaw had gone home from the funeral and something like four hundred pots of gut-tanning tea were being brewed behind gritstone walls at this very moment. Few people were about in the streets, and as Mosley came within sight of the windows of Aitken, Henderson and Brigg, old Teddy Bemrose came out of their front door with such timeliness that he might possibly have been watching for him.

"Could I have a moment of your time, Mr. Mosley?"

Teddy Bemrose's speech had a touch of the archaic about it, heavily aspirated, every consonant sounded. The time was long past when a Bradburn firm of solicitors had considered it worth their while to maintain a full-time office in Upper Crudshaw. Nowadays it was open on two half-days a week for building society, mortgage and rent-book business, at other times for professional consultation by appointment only. One of the partners would come out to deal with Crudshaw's divorces, conveyancing, defence against traffic summonses and civil wars between neighbours. Routine work (together with the free issue of a good deal of strictly unofficial but highly competent advice) was performed by old Teddy, a managing clerk who manned part-time branch-offices in three other villages on other days of the week. It followed that what Mosley did not know, old Teddy often did; and if it came to buying one piece of confidential information with another, both men had docile professional consciences.

"If you wouldn't mind just stepping inside for a minute, Inspector Mosley."

Outside, if there was the slightest danger that the most innocuous syllable might be overheard, old Teddy was a stickler for protocol. In the dusty, chilly, legal squalor of his office it was *Nah, Teddy—Nah, Jack—*

Bemrose was a thin man, unfleshed to the point of scragginess. His suit was of a cut that had been beginning to look old-fashioned in 1939, but this was an image that he clearly aimed to foster. He added to it the focal point of a narrow stiff collar whose wings cradled a bony knob of Adam's apple. The oval lenses of his bi-focal spectacles glinted as if reflecting their wearer's prudence and treble-checking care.

"I've had it in mind to show you this for some months

now, Jack. It goes without saying that I shouldn't, but I've hardly slept these last few nights for thinking of what might have been different if I had. And yet I don't know."

Teddy Bemrose's pronouncements often ended with his not knowing. Mosley knew better than to try to rush him.

"Then of course I've no cause to be laying the blame at my own door."

Bemrose sifted about in a pile of papers and brought out a common building society pass-book, which he handed to Mosley without comment. Mosley looked unexcitedly through its pages, especially the earlier and later ones.

"One thousand, two hundred and fifty pounds—that's a lot of money for a man like Reuben Tunnicliffe to have saved—with the size of family that he's sent out into the world."

"He was a very careful man," Bemrose said. "When he did come in here to make a withdrawal, he always used to behave as if he thought it was something improper he was doing—as if he was offending both me and the society by taking his own money out. And what do you make of those withdrawals, Jack?"

"There's a big one here, eighteen months ago: five hundred quid. How did he take it? A warrant payable to somebody?"

"Cash. Twenty pound notes, mostly. Of course, I had to ask for notice. I don't keep any big sums in the safe here that I don't have to. Reuben hadn't a bank account. He didn't like cheques. He had to scout about for someone to cash them for him—and that meant letting an outsider know his affairs."

"Did he let on what he wanted it for?"

"He did not. And each time there was something in his eye that said don't ask."

"Yes—each time. I see this happened regularly."

Mosley did mental arithmetic with the dates.

"Almost but not quite every three months. First five hundred. Then two-fifty. Then two hundred. Then twice it was fifties. Going down all the time. Well, it had to, hadn't it? Ending up with a balance of twelve pounds thirty-eight pence. And the last withdrawal was a good five months ago. According to the pattern, there'd have been another by now—if there'd been anything left worth taking. I saw nothing new in his house just now. Where was it all going, Ted? What's your feeling?"

"Well, I don't know," Bemrose said. "Some of the possibilities could of course be harmless."

"Such as helping one of his youngsters out of a difficulty."

"He always vowed he'd never do that. Said they all had to be treated alike, and if he hadn't enough to help them all out of holes, he'd help none."

"And yet, Ted, a lot of these old-timers are given to barking worse than they bite. If one of the young Tunnicliffes really was up against it—"

"I don't think that's it, Jack. If it was money to be sent out of Crudshaw, it would have been a case for a crossed warrant. He might have sounded a little simple, Jack. His sort do. I meet a lot of them in this office. They think looking a bit daft is a kind of defence. Reuben Tunnicliffe had his head screwed on all right. He was a man who didn't always look as if he was listening—but he was."

Mosley used a pipe-charging ritual to tide him over another change of thought.

"He was an old man, Ted, and he knew he wasn't getting any younger. Maybe he wanted cash in the house, so that if anything happened to him, Annie would be covered— and the probate people wouldn't know how much he was leaving."

"I'd say he was far too shrewd for that. He had a will properly drawn up by us. Mr. Henderson went into all the facts and figures with him. There wasn't enough there to interest the taxman. Reuben knew that."

"So?"

"I just don't know, Jack."

"There's a nasty thought hanging about at the back of my mind, Teddy. It looks as if he was paying money regularly to somebody. Then he goes and hangs himself when a quarterly instalment is getting badly overdue. What did Reuben Tunnicliffe ever do that he might have to pay somebody to keep quiet about it?"

"He's a man I'd have trusted anywhere. I'd have left him in here with my safe open. He wouldn't have cheated at a fruit and vegetable show. But you never know, with folk, do you, Jack?"

"I'll turn this all over in my mind, Teddy."

"You do that, Jack. And of course, I haven't said a word—"

"Ta-ta, Teddy."

"Ta-ta, Jack."

Chapter Three

There were certain categories of crime that were not condemned as universally in Mosley's country as some absolute moralists might have preferred. Poaching, for example, within the modest domestic requirements of an otherwise reasonably honest man, was regarded on Hadley Fell as the small tradesmen of Bradburn might consider a mistake in their favour by the Inland Revenue. It was a small bonus that one accepted, as it were, without kicking up a fuss. One certainly did not draw HM Inspector's attention to his error.

There was one offence, however, that paralleled the theft of a companion's horse in the frontier epoch of Western America, and that was the misappropriation of another man's sheep. It happened that at the time of Reuben Tunnicliffe's suicide there was an epidemic of sheep-rustling that had about it all the visible and outward signs of professional management. Some days passed before Mosley was able to give further active attention to affairs in Upper Crudshaw: he was seconded to reinforce the sheep-protecting resources of another division.

And during this period, he comported himself in an atypically quiet and conformist manner. They had quasimilitary conferences, much beloved by those top-floor gentlemen who regretted their missed chances as masterminds behind the lines of war. (One of them even referred to the meetings he convened as *O Groups*.)

It is hardly likely that Mosley believed in every basic strategy that was propounded at these meetings, but he sat through them without offering interruption and accepted compliantly the tasks allotted to him. One of these involved a night operation of the kind that made some men wonder why they had become and remained policemen. It was all because a fairly newly promoted detective-sergeant in P division had used his eyes at Bradburn cattle market. He had noticed a livestock-transporting vehicle in the car park, and it was clear from the state of its floor that it had not recently transported livestock. But neither did it collect any. At the end of the morning's business it was still there, with out-of-town registration plates and no crew whom one could positively have identified as being in charge of it. Not until late in the afternoon, when pens were being swilled down, and the farmers who had been critically watching the auction had gone off to take advantage of the liberally extended licensing hours, did two men appear from nowhere and drive the vehicle away empty. The proprietor's name had been painted out from the sides of the truck, but a check had already been made with Department of Transport records and showed it to belong to a hiring contractor who would be certain to disclaim any knowledge of the intentions of his hirers.

Detective-Sergeant Merrill radioed in his intentions, and was given HQ's blessing as he drove after it through Stopeley in the general direction of Cowburn. It was deep in the hill country near there, neatly tucked away in the grounds of a derelict gravel-working, that the wagon came to rest and the crew brewed up and deployed their bedrolls.

Merrill observed all this without giving his presence away and was told to remain where he was, reporting back only if the vehicle moved. The spot was flagged on a portentous operations map at HQ as the likely start-line for a new sortie by the rustlers, who had so far never struck in the same place twice.

Mosley was put in charge of a small task force to keep tabs on the gravel-pit and deployed his minions without emotion and without expressing any views of his own about the tactics wished on him by other men. Dusk and a light rain descended on the gravel-pit more or less simultaneously. Darkness and rain intensified together. A northeasterly wind rose a couple of points on the Beaufort scale. There was no shelter available that could be taken without relaxing vigilance. Mosley turned his raincoat collar up about his neck and chin. He made several rounds of his outposts, with whom his sole conversation was sufficient whispering to make sure they were still awake.

An hour after dawn, rain and wind began to slacken.

The driver of the van woke up and roused his mate. Warm and dry in the back of their truck, they packed up their bedding and it was at this stage, following his orders, that Mosley approached them. They told him that they had spent yesterday at Bradburn market, but the dealer to whom they were under contract had bought no animals. So they had driven up into the country for a cheap and quiet night. Did Mosley know of a transport pull-up where they could get a mug of tea and a bacon sandwich? Mosley did, and after checking their papers and everything about their vehicle that lent itself to being checked, sent them on their way.

A dozen sheep vanished that night from the lower slopes of a fell ten miles away from where Mosley had been watching. There seemed no way of accounting for how this had been managed.

There then followed a temporary lull in rustling on wet nights. The force reverted to its normal deployment and Mosley was able to spend a couple of days in places like Hadley Dale and Hayburn Market, where he generally reckoned to hear enough to keep him abreast of the state of his empire. Information came his way in urinals, on draughty bus-station seats—even in public reading rooms, where speech was theoretically forbidden. It was from a pair of Crudshaw biddies, returning from a closing down sale at Renwick, that he first heard of Annie Tunnicliffe's new lease of life.

"I don't know where she gets her energy from."

"Dressed to the nines at the Bingo last Friday, she was. Looked like a fiddler's bitch, my husband said."

"Aye. But that's not all. I hope I'm past certain things by the time I'm her age."

"Some people never seem past it. And she must be in good training after old Reuben."

"But don't you think it's disgusting, old people like that?"

"I don't see why it should be."

"Oh, I do. The skin flaking off their chests, and their arms and legs looking as if they were famine victims—and then to do that—"

"My old man'll be doing it until his what-not drops off. And even then, he'll think of summat."

"No, but don't you reckon old Reuben kept her down too much?"

"Well, if she wasn't down, he'd never have got anything up, would he?"

They screamed with laughter.

"Well, Percy Darwent's after her, that's for sure. Her eighty-one and him sixty-seven! I reckon it's a question of which'll wear the other out first. They say he's been sweet on her half his life."

"Percy Darwent and others. He's been seen coming away from hers at all hours. Sammy Walton's another. Caleb Bilson. My God—I wouldn't fancy it with Caleb, would you? I wonder what he does with that iron he wears on his leg, when he's on the nest? Of course, it may be only Annie's twenty-three inch colour telly they're going to see. She's been spending money like a woman with no arms."

It was Thursday afternoon, so Mosley knew that it was Teddy Bemrose's day for collecting his dues and dispensing desiccated wisdom from behind his dusty desk in Earl's Pottle.

"I gather things are looking up on Annie Tunnicliffe's horizons, Ted."

"Oh, aye. The best turn Reuben ever did her was hanging himself, it seems."

"Every eligible widower in Upper Crudshaw putting down his stake-money, I'm told."

"Aye—that's if the word eligible is made of elastic. They're making a book on it in the Stonewrights' Arms, I'm informed. But the way the odds keep jumping about, there must be a lot of hedging going on. Last Friday, Sammy Walton turned up for the Bradburn bus wearing Reuben's Sunday overcoat, and that brought him down to evens. But then Percy Darwent was seen in Reuben's boots, and carrying Reuben's umbrella, whereupon he became favourite overnight. Mind you, it appears you have to be careful how you talk about these things in the Stonewrights', because Annie's in there every night herself except Wednesdays. That's her evening class."

"Evening class?"

"Beginners' Italian. She confided in Mrs. Foden that she

thought it might give her the opportunity to meet a better class of person."

"Spending heavily, is she? In the pub, for example?"

"Not as far as I know. I've heard no stories of her taking too much, and it seems she's very mean about treating."

"That's something that even a fortune wouldn't cure her of. Did Reuben leave her any other money besides the twelve pounds he had left in your building society?"

"He'd once been paid out in shares by a small-time football pool that was having cash-flow problems. We hope to realize something like five pounds on them—but it will be some time before it comes through."

"I'm still not happy about something, somewhere, Teddy. There's nobody else started making regular withdrawals, I hope?"

"No. But of course the society we represent is not the only form of investment open to Upper Crudshaw."

"I suppose not."

And that thought, or something arising close from it, seemed to give Mosley a fresh idea. As he sat opposite Bemrose, in the run-down office lined with its shelves of legal tomes that no one would surely ever open again, a wide smile suddenly spread across the lower half of his face. It was not that Mosley's smiles were all that infrequent. He was incorrigibly conservative about the company that he permitted to see them.

"I've thought of something, Teddy. This needs clearing up, and I think I see a way of getting to the bottom of it. Mind you, I shall need a fair amount of co-operation in Crudshaw—including yours."

"You know you can rely on me, Jack."

"What I really need is the loan of your Crudshaw office telephone, if you wouldn't mind taking a few incoming calls for me."

"Of course, Jack. Anything you ask."

But he did not tell Teddy Bemrose what the calls were going to be about. Teddy listened and nodded. All he had to do was name a few likely racehorses to inquiring punters. It was only after Mosley had gone that he had second thoughts. Mosley was a good man. He knew his way about the hills. But did any man who was in possession of his wits ever become involved in any of his schemes? In particular, was undercover work for Mosley in any way fitting for a solicitor's managing clerk?

Teddy Bemrose supposed it would be all right. He did not foresee the sleepless nights he had ahead of him.

Chapter Four

The vicar of Upper Crudshaw, the Reverend Wilfred Weskitt, was a young man, though not as young as he looked. No man could be as young as Wilfred looked and be allowed to operate as a vicar. His wife, Cindy, was younger still and even less ecclesiastical than she looked. When the Weskitts had first come to Crudshaw, some four years ago, the innovatory spirits of Wilfred and Cindy had offended a few members of the congregation and caught the fancy of a few outsiders. Three had left and three had joined, maintaining the attendance at all but the more spectacular services at an average of about ten.

It was on the Reverend Weskitt that Mosley paid his first call when he got back to Upper Crudshaw. He and Wilfred Weskitt had already done business together over a case of graveyard vandalism which for various reasons could not be brought to court. One of those reasons had been that there might have been parental complaints about two thick ears and one broken nose that the vicar had visited upon the offenders. And Mosley had so confused the evidence that no case had been presentable on that issue, either.

Wilfred Weskitt was not in when Mosley called. He had been bidden to Bradcaster to justify to his venerable archdeacon a paragraph of dubious theological tenability in the most recent edition of his parish magazine.

Mosley was therefore received by Cindy, a disturbing experience for any man who retained as much as a distant memory of hormone activity. For Cindy Weskitt was candid about her sexual endowments and patently aware of the effect that they had on anyone with anything viable inside his trousers. Moreover, she overtly enjoyed the discomfort that she strewed about her, secure in the knowledge that her heart belonged exclusively to Wilfred.

And some people found even this odd, for there were basic things that she did not share with the vicar. She was a disbeliever. She was an argumentative agnostic. She had

once propounded her views at a diocesan Brains Trust that
was so sensationally publicized that Wilfred had had to
acknowledge them from his pulpit, telling his thirty-five
listeners (it was Easter Sunday) that it was an astringent
privilege to live in contention with such cogently tempting
rationalism. At the end of the day, of course, he reminded
the uncomprehending faces, it was the final triumph of
Faith over glittering epigram. The worshippers—thirty of
them were women—went on with their spiritual exercises
in comparative millinery.

Cindy Weskitt sat with Mosley on her sofa; close to Mosley on her sofa. Her Chanel caused even Mosley's phleg-
matic senses to swim. He looked steadily in front of himself.

"Reuben Tunnicliffe—" he said.

"That poor man. Do you know there was a commotion
in the parochial church council about burying him in con-
secrated ground?"

"I'd wondered about that."

"I told Wilf I'd leave him if he didn't see to it that Reuben
Tunnicliffe was planted with due deference."

"I didn't think you attached all that much importance to
ritual," Mosley said.

"I don't. But Wilf has to. It's his job. It's his job to see
to it that people get the last ounce of comfort out of what
they believe in."

"Well—that's a point of view."

"Look," she said, the warmth of her shoulder penetrating
through Mosley's jacket. "It's all a question of illusion. Where
two or three are gathered together under a satisfying illusion, it's a pastoral priority to nourish that illusion. It's the
only hope the poor sods have got."

"Reuben Tunnicliffe was under an illusion. He was under
the illusion that he could no longer tolerate his own existence."

"Yes. That's puzzled me. I didn't know him well. But I'd
seen him about, chatted him up a time or two. A man who
enjoyed himself in his peculiar way, I'd have thought—and
expected to go on doing so."

Though perhaps he knew he would never realize the full
potential that the vertiginous nearness of Cindy Weskitt
must have put into his mind.

"We think he was being blackmailed," Mosley said.

"Blackmailed? Reuben Tunnicliffe? What about, for God's sake?"

"That remains to be discovered."

"By somebody local?"

"I think it is bound to have been. Reuben cannot have trespassed all that far afield."

"I don't think I have ever heard of anything so—so base, Mr. Mosley."

"That was why I was hoping you would play a little part for me. I am determined to nail this villain. We have an expression in the Force. We call it mixing a man a bottle."

"I am not a dispensing chemist, but I am always open to learn new arts."

So Mosley told her how he hoped it would work out, and when he had finished, she laughed. It was the kind of laughter that it was a joy to have set off.

"There is only one thing, Mrs. Weskitt. I may be going away for a short while."

"On holiday, Mr. Mosley?"

"That is in the lap of my superiors—or will be, when I put it to them."

"So while you're away—?"

"If I might ask you to keep a weather eye on progress for me—to keep things gently rolling, as it were—"

"Oh what a joy you are, Mr. Mosley."

Cindy Weskitt was still laughing when they heard the Reverend Weskitt taking his shoes off in the hall. He did not look as if he would easily be made merry by his wife's abandon. The archdeacon had not been in a listening mood.

"I am helping Mr. Mosley to mix a man a bottle," his wife said.

Millicent Millicheap was Upper Crudshaw's poet, though her work was not to be found in any anthology. She had in her time written a memorable line or two, and also a few that were comprehensible—but never one that was both at the same time. But she was perceptive, prolific and drunkenly in love with words. Poetry had become her life. Everything she encountered was a potential line of poetry. She saw everything in terms of something else. She identified with everything and everybody. Her empathy was so universal and so unflagging that it was a wonder she could bear to live in a world so full of potential agony. It could only be that the tumbling of words from her brain and pen was enough to assuage her every conflict. Her verse was seldom printed and even less frequently read; but Upper Crudshaw had no other poet, so was quite proud to accept that she was one.

Millicent Millicheap was vague, possessed barely the means on which to subsist, and suffered from delusions of grandeur on a peculiarly unmeaningful (and harmless) plane. For example, she had been known to advertise in the *personal* column of the London *Times* her quite good but frankly very ordinary home-made green tomato chutney.

Millicent Millicheap would not have been every detective inspector's choice as confidential agent in an undercover operation of questionable legality, especially one that might go very badly wrong while he expected to be away. But she appealed to Mosley for several reasons. One was that she was the spokesman of the underdog *par excellence*. She would happily throw herself behind any minority cause in the world, needing only to be persuaded that it was a minority cause. Her enthusiasm—at least initially—was always unlimited. Moreover, she did not care about other people's opinions of her, which never seemed to come to her ears anyway. There were possible outcomes of *Exercise Tunnicliffe* that were destined to interfere with Teddy Bemrose's sleep. But Mosley was not in the least worried about the consequences that he might be letting Millicent Millicheap in for. She was unlikely even to be aware of them.

When Mosley knocked at Miss Millicheap's door, she had on a pale green granny-length knitted woollen frock and her hair was untidy. She knew, apparently, about the French roll, and had gone some way towards producing one. Her most striking feature, however, were the Wellington boots that she was wearing about the house. She was capable of not knowing what she had put on her feet this morning.

"Reuben Tunnicliffe, Miss Millicheap—"

"Ah, yes. Very sad. He always reminded me, you know,

of an ant-eater. I can't think why. I always used to say to myself: here comes the ant-eater."

"Suicide is always very distressing, Miss Millicheap. So unnecessary."

"Sing ho, sing hey, *Felo de se*—No: that isn't in the best of taste, is it?"

"In Reuben Tunnicliffe's case the unnecessary element is particularly deplorable. I have reason to believe that he was unnecessarily driven to it."

"Poor old ant-eater. But what do you mean, Mr. Mosley?"

"I believe that someone may have been extorting payment from him to keep quiet about some past peccadillo. From what I know of old Reuben, it must have been something pretty trivial; something that seen in perspective probably wasn't worth five old pence of hush money."

"Indeed I am sure you are right, Mr. Mosley. My heart goes out to that poor little wife of his. For some extraordinary reason she always reminds me of a fruit-bat."

"I have come to you, Miss Millicheap, to see if you might be prepared to give me a little unobtrusive help. You are, of course, absolutely free to decline."

"Oh, I never decline. I never decline anything, Mr. Mosley. I've not declined anything since they made me drop Latin at school. They made me do Botany instead."

She laughed outrageously at this absurdity, and when Mosley had finished telling her his plan of battle, she was gleeful with anticipation.

"Oh, what fun this all sounds!"

"I am quite sure, Miss Millicheap, that you will have no cause to be embarrassed by any approach that is made to you. By the nature of this thing, everything will have to be done with the utmost discretion. And I must also ask you not to discuss it with anyone at all. Except the vicar's wife, if she makes contact with you."

"Oh, I shan't. Even if I was tempted to, I should probably forget. I shall put the whole affair out of my mind until the moment comes when I have to send for you in a hurry."

"Perfect! I wish you were a member of our force, Miss Millicheap."

Chapter Five

UCRUFC was not an acronym that naturally caught on and even the members no longer used it, except on their T-shirts. More warmly they were known across the board, by everyone from OAPs to the Play Group, as the Rugger Buggers. Even such custodians of archaic dignity as the Misses Halliburton and the Rev. Evans-Williams, the Baptist Minister, seemed unaware that there ought to be anything blushful in the way the label tripped off their tongues.

It was true that the Buggers played a rough game. It was true that they were noisy on and off the field. When they were in plenary session in the Hanging Gate, they did tend to overlook the fact that anyone else might be hoping to enjoy the amenities of the house. When they arrived back within the municipal boundaries after an away fixture, singing lustily on their coach, the least embarrassing form of self-defence was to feign deafness. But if anything allegedly impossible needed to be done in Upper Crudshaw, the Buggers were there. If someone's optimistic project was proving a slow-starter, the Buggers got it off the ground. If funds had to be raised, the Buggers raised them waylaying passers-by in alarming fancy dress, and organizing lotteries that sailed in the teeth of the law. When free labour was needed on some new community development, the Buggers were on the site with picks and barrows before it had been properly surveyed.

Mosley needed the services of the Rugger Buggers but was too shrewd a man to suggest a muster parade. Willing as the Buggers invariably were, they were apt to reach their own impetuous conclusions before one had finished one's exposition; there was always the danger that they might leap into action before they had learned what action was desired, or where. It was safer to isolate a few of their relative mental giants, to outline one's intentions several times over in varying word-forms, and then to leave one's contacts to translate the scheme into language that would be understood by the pack.

Mosley chose Dicky Umbers, the Upper Crudshaw hooker, Freddy Lowther, their weaselly little fly-half, and Pete Pollitt, their mountainous, crippled, non-playing secretary. Mosley's scenario appealed to them. Dicky Umbers, who could not normally sit down at a table without knocking most of its contents to the floor, laughed so convulsively that the others rushed to safeguard their pints.

"Of course, we're on to a winner with Cindy Weskitt," the secretary said.

"There's nowt much wrong wi't' vicar, for that matter," Umbers said. "Well, we do know what's wrong wi' 'im, don't we, and that's nowt 'e or we can do owt about, is it? And he does nobody any harm."

"Are we to understand, then, Mr. Mosley, that the Reverend Weskitt is going to be in on this from square one?"

"I think we may safely leave that decision to Mrs. Weskitt," Mosley said. "I believe she is fully capable of handling him."

"Aye—but is he capable of handling her?"

"She always looks to me as if she's not getting all she could do with. Wilf Weskitt must have more under his surplice than you see from the front pew."

"When was tha last i't' front pew? Or any pew, for that matter?"

"Gentlemen—" Mosley said.

His three hand-picked Buggers wanted to go into action straight away. They were richly imaginative, rumbustious men, falling over each other already to suggest resources that Mosley himself might never have thought of. He let their enthusiasm flourish unbounded for some minutes. No bad thing for them to be straining in the starting-traps. But eventually he applied gentle restraint.

"Gentlemen—I do not want you to do anything immediate. I am thinking of this as a longish-term policy. We must not rush at things. Upper Crudshaw was not built in a day."

"No—but that's only because they took an extended lunch-break, so as to be sure of overtime. Do we take it, then, Mr. Mosley, that you will be in touch?"

"No. I shall not be in touch. And I do not want you trying to get in touch with me. That could ruin the entire enterprise. You will get your timings from Mrs. Weskitt. I will use her as my liaison officer."

"You crafty old sod."

Horace Kettle, boilerman-caretaker at the council offices, was an old soldier: the sort of old soldier whose crime sheet had been as long as the band of good conduct chevrons that he had worn without authority on his sleeve. Horace never did anything except on receipt of a direct and unambiguous order—and, if then, strictly in his own time. There was only one aspect of his work that the council offices did not complain about. He did keep the boilers stoked: otherwise he would have been cold.

Was Horace Kettle another of those whom it might have surprised an outsider to see Mosley insinuating into a position of subtle trust? There were predictabilities about Horace that appealed to Mosley. Horace was his own boilerman. No man was in Horace's confidence. It had been said of Horace that he played his cards so close to his chest that it was sometimes doubtful whether he had seen them himself. He was totally and exclusively, if not always effectively, self-seeking—and one of the planks in his creed was that it paid him to keep in with the likes of Mosley.

"Nah, Horace."

"Nah, Mr. Mosley."

"I wondered if there was somewhere we could talk?"

There was a cubby-hole in the cosiest corner of the cellars where Horace did his paper work. There were charts on Horace's walls that looked as if they might be prognostic of Upper Crudshaw's economical consumption of combustible fuels. They were in fact an extrapolation from the racing form-book that he claimed was his personal invention. Horace was not anxious for Mosley to enter this office, but Mosley preceded him into it, diplomatically averting his eyes from a wholesale carton of cigarettes that might possibly have changed hands at a price not recommended by its manufacturer.

"You've got it nice and snug down here, Horace."

"Too bloody draughty," Horace said, it being one of his

tenets never to express satisfaction with anything. If nobody ever grumbled, how could you expect anything ever to improve?

"How well did you know Reuben Tunnicliffe, Horace?"

Horace racked his brain for any respect in which Mosley might be trying to bring him to book for what had happened to Reuben.

"Not all that well, Mr. Mosley."

"Pity about him," Mosley said.

"Oh, yes. It put me off my food for the rest of the day, when I heard."

Once he had grasped the official line of thought, Horace could come up smartly alongside.

"Need never have happened," Mosley said.

"No?"

"Being leaned on by some bastard who had something on him."

"Bastard."

"I'm going to nail that bastard, Horace."

"I hope you do, Mr. Mosley."

"You're going to help me, Horace."

Horace did his best not to look uncountenanced by the suggestion. Co-operation with the law went without saying, when one of its craftiest, dodgiest, least trustworthy operators had his horny great forefinger in your buttonhole —but one had to consider the sensitivities of one's friends, if they ever got to hear of it.

"You know me, Mr. Mosley. You've only to ask."

"Have you any buckshee space down here where you could do a bit of storage for me, Horace?"

His eye strayed in the direction of the cigarette-carton, but he did not seem to take it in: not this time round.

"Storage space, Mr. Mosley? Well, there, if I may say so, you couldn't have come to a better man."

There couldn't be too much trouble in that, as long as he watched points: though he wouldn't care for Mosley to go poking too conscientiously round every basement corner at this very moment. A home elsewhere would have to be found for one or two of Horace's recent acquisitions.

"What sort of stuff was it that you had in mind, Mr. Mosley? Is there a lot of it?"

"Bales," Mosley said. "Sewn up in sacking. Some people might mistake them for sheep's fleeces."

Oh yes. Horace had heard they were having recalcitrant sheep trouble over up Cowburn way: changes of ownership that hadn't been agreed with slapped hands. It sounded like syndicated crime by the scale of it. He could not think why Mosley would want to bring loot down here. He was well known for working round corners, Mosley was. But surely to God he wasn't bent?

"Not more than four dozen of them at the most," Mosley added.

Four dozen? Forty-eight? Forty-eight baled up bloody sheep's fleeces? What did he think this was? Bloody Harrods?

"I don't think I could manage that, Mr. Mosley."

"Pity. I'd been relying on you."

"It wouldn't leave me room to turn round, Mr. Mosley."

Nor would it. Horace could see himself having to lug a bale out of the way every time he wanted to swing a shovel at his fire-door.

Mosley began to look about the little office, sniffing his way along the shelves like a cat in a forbidden cupboard. As if casually, he picked up the box of cigarettes, ran his thumb-nail along one of its sealed flaps.

"Did you know they print a number under here, Horace, so that it's possible to trace exactly where a consignment has come from?"

"No, I didn't know that, Mr. Mosley. Is that so?"

Horace sounded bright and naively interested.

"I suppose they have to do that, seeing the sort of people there are about these days. I buy these wholesale from a man in the trade, you know. All legitimate and above board. It's better than having to keep going out in this east wind for a packet of ten, every time I want a drag."

"I'm sure it is. You don't think I'm worried about these, do you? But these sheep's fleeces, Horace—"

"I'll think of something, Mr. Mosley."

"I'll tell you what: I'll try and make it not more than two or three at a time."

What the hell was this? What the blazes was Mosley playing at? There was a difference between forty-eight and two or three. Come to think of it, even two or three were going to be a full-time handful.

"When will they be coming, Mr. Mosley?"

"I can't say."

"You'll be having a word with them upstairs, just to keep me in the clear?"

"No. I don't want anyone else to know a thing about this, bar you and me. Not even them upstairs."

"What—not the chairman? Not Mr. Barraclough?"

"Nobody, Horace. This is between you and me, until further notice. And if anybody comes sneaking up threatening you—well, then you get on to me at once, and on the quiet."

Threatening him? Horace Kettle distinctly preferred a world in which he was not likely to be threatened. He licked his bloodless lips.

"I think you see what I'm getting at, don't you, Horace."

"Oh yes. I know what you're getting at, Mr. Mosley. You couldn't have come to a better man."

Chapter Six

It was two or three weeks before anyone in Upper Crudshaw saw Mosley again. He ambled over his sparsely populated territory in typical fashion—as some junior CID wag put it, Mosleying about—paying calls that bore no visible relationship with any case-work that he was known to have on at the moment, and of which no memoranda ever reached those to whom he was accountable. One such visit was to Nelson Brindley, a one-eyed hill-farmer who saw him coming while he was still half a mile away, and was therefore able to make adjustments to the position of certain machinery in his yard.

"Nah, Nelson."

"Nah, Jack."

Nelson's eye restlessly travelled up and down Mosley's face. He was never quite sure where the interest of an unexpected caller might lie, and by the same token, callers like Mosley were never certain what Nelson was anxious to hide on any particular occasion.

"Canst tha sell me a fleece, Nelson?"

Nelson knew very well that he could, but it was one of his principles never to agree with anything without first pleading almost superhuman difficulties. Eventually, the sale was agreed.

"And canst tha have it delivered to Upper Crudshaw council offices basement, care of Horace Kettle?"

Nelson was most unsure what signal he was seeing this time.

"Seems a rum do, that," he said.

"Wheels within wheels within wheels, Nelson."

"Well, if tha says so, Mr. Mosley. I shall have to charge thee for transport, of course."

It went without saying that the fleece would be delivered with the maximum secrecy and precaution. Everything Nelson Brindley did, he did as if it were illegal.

* * *

In the meanwhile, the rustling of sheep from the high-lying moorlands continued to appear insoluble, particularly since Chief Inspector Marsters had been put in charge of the counter-operation. As many as twenty animals had been known to have been spirited away in a single night—and invariably from some corner remote from the spot where Marsters's highly select network of informants had confidently told him to expect the next strike. One notable exception had been another wet and windy night when Marsters and a veritable posse had clung to such lee as was afforded by a disgracefully ill-maintained wall, plotting over the brow the headlamps of what could only have been an illicit sheep-transporter. A ram and eight ewes had disappeared that night from a field not a quarter of a mile behind Marsters's back.

Marsters had come into this range-war with all the swash-buckling verve of an undercover US marshal about to expose the deficiencies of a rye-sodden county sheriff. Once, when he told one of his sergeants to take two men and head a suspicious stranger off at the top of a valley, he had to glower to suppress the tittering. And the next morning, when he came to get his greatcoat from a peg in Stopeley Police Station, he found that someone had pinned to its lapel a five-pointed star made from kitchen foil.

But the assignment of CI Marsters to write a final *finis* to the sheep-stealing wave did relieve Mosley, at least for the time being, of nights in the bracken, peering out into the hearts of the Pennine storms. There was no way in which Marsters would have consented to lead a team of which Mosley was a member. Marsters took it as a personal affront that Mosely drew his salary cheque from the same county treasurer as himself, and for what appeared on the surface to be not dissimilar duties. Once, Marsters had come very close indeed to shopping Mosley: or thought he had. Since then, Detective-Superintendent Grimshaw, who had a grudging and elaborately qualified respect for Mosley, had needed every last resort of ingenuity to keep the two officers apart.

Then one morning, when Marsters's range-riding was

beginning to wear down a good many others in addition to himself, and the affairs of Upper Crudshaw were so static that Grimshaw had forgotten the existence of the place, Mosley asked his detective-superintendent's secretary for an interview.

There was something odd about Mosley's attitude. Mosley had more than one habitual mode of approach to the man whose orders he was supposed to obey, and Grimshaw had long since learned not to take any of them at their face-value. If Mosley was going out of his way to be polite, then he was trying to divert attention away from something. If he was beng positively respectful, then he was about to seek approval for some tactic that deviated monstrously from anything that the Police and Public Order Committee would conceivably stomach. If he was endeavouring to appear ingenuously honest, then the stability of the entire force must surely be under some hidden threat.

But today Mosley was not himself. He was embarrassed. He was coy. He could not look Grimshaw in the eye. He did not like fashioning the phrases that he had come here to speak. For once, Grimshaw did not think that Mosley was acting.

"Sit down, Jack. Not smoking?"

He hadn't given up his pipe, had he, for God's sake? Grimshaw did not think that he would be able to carry on in office, if life were further complicated by a Mosley suffering from withdrawal symptoms.

"No, Tom—well you see—it's like this—My wife—"

Mosley's family saw so little of him that it often came as a surprise to younger members of the Force that he had one. Mosley's wife played hardly any part in his vocational life. Those who had not met her rather naturally assumed that there was a sourness between them which made it a relief to both parties that he did spend so much of his time wandering inclement hills in the service of the unwritten legal code that governed the rural peace. But twice a year Mrs. Mosley put in an appearance, to *get her mark* at the two social functions that Mosley attended in his pre-war evening dress: the police ball and the annual bun-fight at which the Chief exchanged excruciating small-talk with his officers, and where ambitious men on their way up dropped

crafty reminders about any achievement that they feared
he might have missed. Mrs. Mosley was then discovered
to be a rotund and jolly little woman, who remained close
to her husband's elbow and evinced such abysmal ignorance
of all police matters that she could get away with remarks
that from any less genial tongue could have gone on indelible record as irreparable insults.

"Yes: how is Marian, Jack?"

"Oh very well. Yes, very well indeed, thank you, Tom.
Over the moon, in fact, I think the current saying goes.
You see, she has just—"

And Mosley went on to confess that his wife had entered
a slogan for a competition organized by the makers of her
preferred detergent, for which she had been awarded a
holiday for two on the Costa del Sol.

"And what," Grimshaw asked, cruelly guessing that this
was one of the obstacles to Mosley's fluency this morning,
"was her slogan?"

Mosley swallowed, looked down at Grimshaw's blotter,
on which the D-S had done a rapid pen-and-ink sketch of
a dagger dripping blood.

"Come along, Mosley. Don't keep it to yourself."

Mosley did not squirm. Still looking down, he maintained
the round-shouldered rigidity of a man managing not to
squirm.

"*I'm all white, Jack,*" he said.

Grimshaw trumpeted with laughter. It more than made
his day. It neutralized every drip of acid rain aggro that
had been penetrating his defences for a week. The moment
Mosley left him, he would be through to the ACC. It would
be worth both their whiles going up to share a biscuit with
the Chief. When the day-shift went off duty, there would
be a note on the desk-sergeant's pad to be passed on to his
relief.

"Well, of course, you must go, Jack."

"It may not be all that easy. The dates—"

Mosley was not accustomed to taking his holidays in chunks.
He preferred more frequent short spells. Mosley on holiday
was a minor local legend. He did not seem to know what
to do with leave. He had been known to come back early,
on the grounds that a bathroom that he had thought would

take four days to decorate had only needed two. He had been known to turn up without notice in the middle of a leave and apprehend some villain who had been believed to be at the other end of the country. He had been known to spend a leave not in, but on the fringes of his area, pricking up his ears in inns that he normally did not have the occasion to visit. In the course of one memorable campaign he had used his leave as a weapon in his armour. Disappearing on a standby flight to Nairobi had been one of the factors that led to the breaking of the case.

"In case you are thinking—"

Mosley opened his wallet and brought out the letter from the soap company. Grimshaw made no pretence that he was reading it properly.

"My dear chap, you don't think, surely, after all these years, that I mistrust you? No, of course you must go. Leave rosters exist to be amended. What would we do if you had to appear in court for a fortnight? I can just picture you wallowing in Spanish sunshine while the first glacier of the season is beginning to slither down Hadley Dale. It's you that's all white, Jack: make the most of your dinghy."

The Assistant Chief Constable was still laughing. He exploded at illogical intervals throughout the ensuing conversation.

"What arrangements are you going to make, Tom?"

"Nothing much ever happens on Mosley's patch. At least, nothing ever *need* happen. I thought I'd cover the area myself."

"You know I'm never in favour of generals leading platoons into action, Tom."

What he meant was that he always hated his detective-superintendent to be out of the office. Questions that he could not answer were apt to be referred direct to him.

"The trouble is, I'm only left with Marsters. And I reckon there are another two reels yet before he'll be ready to ride off into the sunset with Hank, Slim and Tex hanging from the oak on Stopeley Green."

"Do him good to have a change of scene. He's beginning to smell of sheep-dip."

"Sir—you know what's likely to happen if I let Marsters loose on Mosley's manor."

"Tom, we can't conduct this force for ever with an eye to accommodating two officers who can't get on together."

"As far as I'm concerned, it's the only way of conducting this force. If Mosley thinks that Marsters is taking over from him, he won't go to Spain."

"All white—ha-ha-ha!—announce that you're taking over, then switch to Marsters when you've checked that the Mosleys' flight has taken off with them aboard."

"And will you personally, sir, guarantee to negotiate a cease-fire after Mosley gets back?"

"You're getting altogether too fidgetty, Tom. Can't you get your wife to write somebody a slogan?"

Mosley in the Med—it was a joy ride for all ranks. Constables burst into hilarious shrieks as they tested shop-door handles in dank shadows: at the image of Mosley prostrate under a southern palm, perhaps bare-chested, but surely not discarding his homburg. A detective-sergeant almost blew an ambush at the unbidden thought of Mosley in stiff collar and black tie forking up his first paella under an umbrella on the *playa*. What would Mosley make of flamenco dancers? What inspirations would he import on his return? A four-foot sombrero next time he umpired for Bradburn Second? A sudden shout of *Olé* as the bowler's arm was silhouetted against the sight-screen?

"A slogan for soap!"

Marsters, when he was told, did not make any *all white* jokes. That would have been showing some sort of sympathy with Mosley.

"You know damned well, Tom, that I'm up to my chin in sheep-droppings."

"That's how I felt about you," Grimshaw said. "There'll be altogether less lanoline in the air over on Mosley's acreage. Nothing much ever happens there."

"You mean nothing is ever brought to light there," Marsters said. "He's too busy pretending he's Old Moore."

"That's just what I mean, Marsters. Mosley's ways are

not yours or mine. But we don't get a lot of trouble out of Mosley's sheikhdom. I'd like it to stay that way for just two weeks. I'd prefer you to take nominal responsibility and stay right away from the area unless something unavoidable comes in."

"That I will give you my word I shall do. I dare not—I dare not—"

Marsters dicing with apoplexy was Marsters at his happiest.

"I dare not drop on my hands and knees to sniff the gutters of Mosley's back alleys for fear of what I might unearth there. I am quite sure that I could find enough in two hours to keep two thirds of this force occupied for a month. And you do realize, don't you, Grimshaw, that the domestic sheep is in danger of extinction in an area that depends on the species?"

Grimshaw had spoken casual words, but they were to become historic. Within forty-eight hours of the Mosleys' departure from Gatwick, something unavoidable did come in from Upper Crudshaw.

Chapter Seven

Chief Inspector Marsters was nostalgically unaffected by the *Auld Lang Syne* tea-caddy, or by the biscuit-tin in the shape of a pre-Raphaelite lantern. Nor for that matter had he any natural sympathy for the wispy little woman whose greatest achievement in life so far appeared to have been to have reached the age of eighty-one. She had mentioned that feat even before she had started telling him about the crime against her. He was familiar with the pattern of senile gullibility.

"You say you had five hundred pounds in the house? Might I ask where you kept it?"

"Up and down," she said. "Here and there."

Obviously she was not prepared to trust him as she had trusted the man who had made off with her money.

"There are such things as banks," Marsters said.

"I don't trust banks."

"You'd as well have trusted a bank as the man you did trust. How much more ready cash have you got about the place?"

Annie Tunnicliffe's lips were tightly pursed, but she saw that she had to answer.

"Not all that much."

"How much?"

"About three hundred."

"Take my advice and get it into the Post Office. Now this man. You got his name from a matrimonial agency, I take it?"

Annie Tunnicliffe shook her head.

"Wouldn't have anything to do with places like that. Never know where you stand with places like that."

Some people never cease to marvel at the capacity of mankind for being conned. Marsters did not marvel. He wearily accepted it. And what did a decrepit old woman like this want with looking for a fresh partner, and her previous one barely two months in his grave? He would have wondered how she had come by a sum like five hundred, but her pride had insisted that she tell him this, even before she had admitted she had lost it. Lost it? She'd given it away, the crack-brained old faggot.

"Co-op dividends," she had said. "I've never spent a penny of them for years."

"I didn't think they still gave dividends. I thought they gave stamps."

"I'm talking about before the war."

"So how did you get to know this man? You answered an advert in the paper, I suppose?"

Mrs. Tunnicliffe looked as if she was not going to answer. Marsters was on the verge of asking her what she had brought him out here for, if she was not going to put him in possession of the facts. But her daughter intervened.

"Come on, now, Mother. You've got to tell Mr. Marsters everything, if you want him to get your money back for you."

Then she herself provided the answer.

"She put her own advert in the *Bradcaster Guardian*, Mr. Marsters."

"Have you kept a copy? May I see it please?"

Home-loving widow, refined, seeks Companion, male; must have health and strength. Permanency possible for clean honest man.

"And this man Passmore replied?"

"Not by letter. He drove up one day in a motor, took me quite by surprise."

"Maroon Cortina with grey roof," the daughter said. "Registration HPP 752C."

Marsters looked at the younger woman for a moment with a disapproving eye. He liked her, if anything, even less than he did her mother. Supposed to be something in the musical world: she looked it—damned great antique comb in her hair, and a bosom like a wet nurse's under a jumper like a knitted sack. From her tone and manner, it looked as if she had positively encouraged her mother in the imbecilities of second childhood.

"Were you here with your mother at this time?" Marsters asked her.

"No. I've been in London, helping a pop group to bring C.P.E. Bach into the twentieth century."

"Why not leave him where he was? Well—we'd better

have the best description your mother can give me of this man."

Marsters always believed in getting a verbal description from complainants before he showed them his albums. This put a pre-set limit on their imagination when they did see the faces of the regulars. There emerged a portrait of a well-preserved late-middle-aged man of smart turn-out and military appearance and expatriate white colonial background. Already a short list was forming in Marsters's mind.

"And what did this man do? He came here a few times, I take it?"

"We went for rides in his motor."

"He took you out for a meal, perhaps?"

"Sometimes."

"Mother!" Susan Tunnicliffe said sharply. "Don't try to hide things. They went off for a dirty week-end, Chief Inspector. At Packer's Hydro, Blackpool North Shore."

She was joking, of course. Family fun between mother and daughter—though it did seem to Marsters that it was a little soon after bereavement to be in any kind of taste.

"Well, don't look so disgusted, Mr. Marsters," Susan Tunnicliffe said. "The human race comes in two basic models. Except for deviants, of which there are none in this family, appetites are roughly the same the world over. It's only table-manners that vary—and some diners do better justice to what's on the menu than others. The genuine gourmet often feels he needs a second helping. My mother has nothing to be ashamed of."

"It's being led up the garden that upsets me," Annie Tunnicliffe said, uneasily, as if she had indeed still preserved some vestigial sense of shame. "I feel, to be quite honest, worse about that than I do about losing the money. I mean, I wouldn't like you to think that I'm a loose woman, Mr. Marsters."

Marsters could not recall any eighty-one-year-old woman whom he had regarded as loose. Not in any active sense, anyway.

"And don't you think a woman is entitled to know what she's getting? I mean, nobody out shopping ought to maul the goods about, but you do have the right to see what you're buying."

"Or have it on appro for a few days," her daughter muttered.

"And on what pretext did he relieve you of five hundred pounds?"

"Well, there I really am ashamed of myself, Mr. Marsters. At my age I ought to have known better. He said he didn't feel free—honourably free, was what he said—to attach himself to me until he had paid off an old debt. He said he was a man who could not sleep soundly in debt."

Marsters decided that if, after retirement, he was ever forced to eke out his pension by confidence tricks, he would never tell any of his victims a reasonable story. They would see through that. He would stick to planes of fantasy. The world's mugs seemed to find them more acceptable.

At this stage he got his sergeant to bring out the albums, and they showed Mrs. Tunnicliffe the portrait gallery. It was amazing how many of those who got themselves immortalized by prison cameras managed to look like escapees from Madam Tussaud's basement. Even Susan, looking over her mother's shoulder, groaned once or twice.

But the old girl managed, without trace of uncertainty, to pick out Willy Barber—who had nearly as many aliases as he had done jobs, and had been inside four times.

"All right, Mrs. Tunnicliffe. I'm not saying we'll pick him up tomorrow, or even next week, but we'll have him, and he's no stranger to where he'll be going. Sergeant Bailey will help you to draw up a statement, and you'll be needed sooner or later to give evidence."

At this juncture someone came to the Tunnicliffes' door, and Susan went to answer it. Left alone with the old woman, Marsters had no line of conversation. He looked at the dismal view from their living-room window: a yard, a barrel, still trailing the relics of last season's frost-bitten nasturtiums, a kennel that had not had a dog in it for years. Mrs. Tunnicliffe was equally stumped for anything to say. Sergeant Bailey helped her to clear a corner of the table and got out statement forms.

When Susan Tunnicliffe came back into the room, it was to say that a woman called Millicent Millicheap had called, having heard that Marsters was in town—news travelled fast in Upper Crudshaw. Would Marsters be so kind as to call on her? She was very worried about something she was supposed to be doing for Inspector Mosley, and she wasn't sure that she was getting things right.

"Upper Crudshaw's poet-in-residence, Mr. Marsters. I'm sure you'll find her entertaining."

"So you're a *Chief* Inspector, Mr. Marsters. I do feel honoured. Does that mean that you can order Inspector Mosley about? It doesn't seem possible, somehow, to think of anybody telling Inspector Mosley what to do."

Well, it had been tried—

"I've done everything Mr. Mosley asked me to, but I can't be sure I've got everything right."

Marsters wondered why Miss Millicheap was wearing Wellington boots in her drawing-room, the left royal blue and the right emerald green. This combination of dual-coloured gumboots had been issued to his workmen by Thomas Barraclough, Two-Faced Tom, the biggest construction engineer in the Brad Valley, and Chairman of the Crudshaw District Council. He hoped that such immediate identification might help to stem the current spate of wholesale thefts from his stores.

"The man's been three times, Mr. Marsters, and he told me the key-words, and I incorporated them in my poems as he told me to, even though they don't make any kind of sense, and some of my regular readers are bound to be perplexed. Look, I'll show you."

She brought out last week's issue of the *Bradcaster Guardian*, whose editor perhaps felt that he was establishing a modest claim to cultural content by filling in the odd inch with gratuitously submitted verse. She folded it open at an inside page.

> The mill-lodge,
> Neutralized like yesteryear's greying treacle,
> Ripples from Zurich to Medicine Hat
> Like wrinkles in a nun's pillow.

"I mean, does it make sense to you, Mr. Marsters? I had to bring *Zurich* and *Medicine Hat* into it somewhere, because those were the key-words Mr. Mosley's friend gave me. Perhaps people will think it was a printer's error."

The only error that that printer had made was in not losing the copy before he set it—

"And this one, you see, the week before, seems even worse every time I read it."

> In sweet-shops long ago,
> Sugar-coated iguanas
> And toffee yellowhammers
> Shimmer on varnished hatpins.

"Anybody knows that iguanas and yellowhammers are never on sale in sweet-shops. And though I'm an occasional believer in random stimulation, I can't help feeling that that was going a bit far. I really do feel that I can't go on with this, Mr. Marsters. What do you think I ought to do?"

"Would you mind beginning at the beginning, Miss Millicheap? This man who comes with key-words—"

"He's from the Site."

"The Site?"

She lowered her voice, as one who is passing a state secret.

"The Early Warning Place on Crudshaw Nab. All those masts and trellised dishes. I wrote a poem about them once. I must show it you before you go."

Time was wasted, Marsters's fingertips drumming the table, while she looked for it. She could not find it.

"Do you know this man's name?"

"No. He explained to me that there's what they call a need-to-know rule, and that I, insignificant little whim of Creation that I am, come into that category. But the other man hasn't been yet."

"What other man?"

"The one that Mr. Mosley said would come. The one who is going to threaten me, and demand money with menaces."

For a woman who was expecting harassment of this order, she sounded quite happily enthusiastic about it.

"Do you think I ought to carry on as I am doing until Mr. Mosley comes back? Should I go on passing the forged coins he gave me? Or would it be better to do nothing?"

"I think on the whole you had better do nothing."

A nutter, he had decided—harmless as long as one gave her a wide enough berth to avoid time-consumption. But there remained one other thing.

"Miss Millicheap—would you mind telling me how you came by those Wellingtons?"

"I bought them at Stead's. Aren't they beautiful?"

She kicked her legs up skittishly.

"I painted them yesterday. You see, I saw two men working on the new Health Centre they're building, and they were wearing boots like these. And I thought to myself, *how cheerful*—what a contribution to the colour-scheme of our drab little town. So I thought that I would do the same. That is where we most need random stimulation, don't you think, Chief Inspector—in the colour-schemes of our drab little town? And whenever those two workmen catch sight of me, they will feel a sense of fellowship, I hope. Don't you think?"

She renewed her efforts to find her poem about the radar bowls. Marsters managed to get away before she could lay her fingers on it.

Then as he came down to where he had parked his car, he saw a figure beckoning him energetically from the office doorway of Messrs. Aitken, Henderson and Brigg: Teddy Bemrose. The Dickensian managing clerk's Adam's apple was positively palpitating as he begged Marsters to come in. News of Marsters's presence must have wild-fired about the town.

"I'm uneasy about things that are happening in this town, Mr. Marsters."

"Oh, indeed?"

"I know it sounds like a cock and bull story—but have you ever come across our local candidate for Parnassus—a Miss Millicheap?"

"I have seen one or two of her pieces," Marsters said cautiously.

"Well, most of the things she writes are over my head. But there is a strange rumour going about the town of late—"

And when he had finished telling the Millicheap story, Bemrose lowered his scaly eyelids and left them lowered for a spell of seconds.

"It's a pity that your Inspector Mosley is not here, Mr. Marsters. He has a quick way of putting his finger on things."

"Mosley is only one cog in a big machine, Mr. Bemrose. You have on call all the resources of a large and skilled force."

"I fear we may need them, Mr. Marsters, because I am going to draw your attention to something else—something very serious indeed: it concerns the vicarage. Again it started as a rumour—but I have heard it from sources that I like to regard as impeccable—from men—and women—who have observed *incidents*."

The Assistant Chief Constable gazed out moodily over the grey slates and miscellaneous cowls that constituted the country view from his office window.

"I wonder how *All White Jack*'s making out, Tom."

"Probably itching to get back to Crudshaw. By the way, I had to send Marsters into his principate this morning. Matrimonial con man—shouldn't take Marsters more than an hour or two."

But at that moment the ACC's secretary spoke in a frightened voice through the intercom. Marsters was demanding immediate audience. Before the ACC could approve of his admittance, Marsters had admitted himself.

There was something about Marsters's appearance that suggested that the day had brought more than he dared ever have prayed for. His large, flat, round face was so red that one looked to see whether it was actually steaming— that is all but the spots above his cheek-bones and his temporal veins, which were purple.

"You didn't tell me that Special Branch have a case going on Mosley's patch."

"If they have, nobody's been fit to tell me about it," Grimshaw said, wondering: unconstitutional things had a habit of happening these days. Professional courtesies were ceasing to be observed all over the country. A detective-superintendent could no longer sleep assured of his unassailability in the middle of his own operational area.

"Tell me," he said, knowing that no power at his command could control the nature of a Marsters narrative.

"Well, if Special Branch aren't involved, they damned

well ought to be. And Mosley, who is mixed up in this up to his ears, damned well knows that."

This was better. It was only Marsters's supposition that Special Branch were active in the area. And this now bore the familiar look of any report by Marsters on the activities of Mosley.

"You'd better tell me about it," Grimshaw said. "As quietly as you can, then we shall be able to see our way into the heart of it."

To his credit, Marsters did make an effort. The effect was similar to the loose-fitting lid of a kettle that is just coming to the boil.

"Are you acquainted with the verse of a Millicent Millicheap?"

"No. I can't say that I am. Of course, I've always been fond of poetry—"

Marsters brought out the two specimens that the Upper Crudshaw laureate had shown him, and planted them aggressively under Grimshaw's eyes.

"Tell me what you make of those."

Grimshaw read them several times.

"Pretty little jingles, I suppose. Words used for words' sake, rather than for any meaning that they might or might not have."

"You think?"

"Well, Zurich and Medicine Hat strike one as being verbal gods from out of the machine. Iguanas and yellowhammers aren't on the bill of fare in the average sweet-shop, and frankly I don't get the bit about the hatpins."

"Precisely. You have a sharp eye, Tom. Those are the key-words. Miss Millicheap says so herself."

"And?"

"They are key-words that she has been told to put in her poems by a man who visits her from the Early Warning Tracking Station on Crudshaw Nab: I need hardly remind you, a highly secret and sensitive installation."

"Granted."

"The poems are then printed in the *Bradcaster Guardian*, presumably for the information of some political undesirable."

"All this sounds a little far-fetched to me, Marsters."

Sometimes, when Marsters wanted to terrify a suspect, he simulated the symptoms of a pending stroke by holding his breath until the veins about his eyes and temples were throbbing to bursting point. He never did care to be doubted.

"What is more, Mosley is privy to all that is going on."

"You think so?" ·

"I know so. He has told Miss Millicheap that she will presently be approached by a man who will attempt to blackmail her, demanding money with menaces."

Tom Grimshaw saw it now. Mosley had left behind him a legpull for Marsters, guessing that the chief inspector would crop up in his area sometime during his absence. But it would not do to tell Marsters that in straightforward terms. That might precipitate a non-simulated stroke.

"Perhaps I'd better go and have a word with this Miss Millicheap," he said.

"Of course, I'd be happy to come with you."

And that was a pity. Grimshaw knew that it would make it very difficult to keep the control of the interview in his own hands. But it was never easy to deny Marsters anything that he passionately desired.

"I'm sure that would be most helpful," he said.

"Because then I'll be able to spot any inconsistencies between what she tells you and what she told me."

"We'll go out tomorrow morning, after conference."

But that was not good enough for Marsters.

"I think we ought to go at once, Tom. If there is anything in this, and if Special Branch do have to be called in—"

Chapter Eight

Rust flakes off old nutmeg graters.
All my old teaspoons are stained with whortleberry juice.
A sliced loaf: *Mother's Pride,*
Falls out of the back of a baker's van
Halfway up Constipation Hill.

Millicent Millicheap was in the throes of composition when Grimshaw and Marsters called. From the catch in her voice she appeared to be not far from tears. She slid her work across the table towards Grimshaw. She used expensive leather-bound manuscript albums as others might use scratch-pads. Even the roughest draft of the creative word, she said, deserved to be treated as sacred.

"There's something about it that I quite like," she said. "It agglomerates improbables, don't you think? But what are people going to make of it? Some of my less sophisticated readers are not going to understand it. I shall lose face."

"Which are the key-words this time?" Grimshaw asked her.

"Practically all of them. *Rust, Flakes. Nutmeg grater. Teaspoons. Whortleberry juice. Mother's Pride. Constipation Hill.* Come to think of it, he practically wrote the whole poem for me this time."

"He? You've seen this man from the Early Warning Tracking Station again?"

"Just now. You've only just missed him. He left about half an hour ago."

"Describe him to me."

"Well, he's—"

She concentrated ferociously, but obviously found it extremely difficult to materialize the man's features.

He was not quite as tall as Mr. Grimshaw, but a little bigger than Mr. Marsters. He wore round spectacles with a very dark frame. He reminded her rather of a sleepy kestrel.

"What age?"

"Between forty and fifty."

"An Upper Crudshaw man?"

"No. They're all strangers, up at the Site."

"Is he a man you've often seen about in Upper Crudshaw?"

"No. The only times I've seen him have been when he's called here."

"Tell me precisely what he asked you to do."

"He just said those words to me: *rust, flakes, nutmeg grater*, and so on—he was very laconic. 'That's your assignment,' he said. 'Try and get the *Guardian* to print your poem this week.' What are people going to think of a poem like that? Suppose someone asks me what it means?"

Suppose someone asked her what any of her poems meant?

"Have you been offered any payment for doing this, Miss Millicheap?"

"No. I'm doing it because Mr. Mosley asked me to."

"Yes. Of course. Mr. Mosley. How long is it since Mr. Mosley made this request?"

"Let me see—three or four weeks. It had to do with Reuben Tunnicliffe."

"Reuben Tunnicliffe?"

"The old man who hanged himself in his outside lavatory."

"Ah, yes, Reuben Tunnicliffe. In what sense has all this to do with Reuben Tunnicliffe?"

"I can't tell you. Mr. Mosley didn't say."

"You do realize that this is a very serious matter, Miss Millicheap? That these messages that you are regularly passing could refer to delicate classified technical data that could be of value to the enemies of this country? And that you may be the one who is actually informing those enemies?"

Out in a mouthful like that, it scared even Grimshaw. Miss Millicheap looked at him wild-eyed. Then she found consolation.

"Oh, but Mr. Mosley wouldn't be involved in anything like that. Of that I feel certain."

Wouldn't he? Surely even Mosley knew better? It was pathetic what confidence Mosley seemed to inspire among his weirdly varied tribe of fans. Suppose the old fool had genuinely come across what he took to be evidence of an offence against national security—surely he knew that not trying to go it alone was the first rule in the book?

Chief Inspector Marsters was sitting with his head back and his flat, oval face almost parallel with the ceiling, a pose he frequently adopted when he wished to make it clear that he was staying out of things. In one way his behaviour throughout this dialogue had been exemplary. He had made no effort to insert himself at all. But Grimshaw found his very presence oppressive. He could feel his colleague's vitriolic criticisms effervescing corrosively inside the man.

This case had to be got to the security people as soon as possible. He had to bring Millicent Millicheap to the attention of Special Branch—even at the risk of being made a laughing-stock by Mosley. Chief Inspector Marsters would die of suppressed emotion if Grimshaw did not make an immediate decision. Millicent Millicheap would have to be taken to Bradburn Station at once.

Grimshaw cleared for action.

"Miss Millicheap—may I see your Wellingtons, please?"

She looked at him with surprise and apprehension, said "Yes, of course," and raised both her heels in the air.

"Miss Millicheap, I have reason to believe that these Wellingtons may be the property of Mr. Thomas Barraclough, building contractor of this town. I must ask you to let me have them, against a receipt, so that I can get them identified."

"This is absurd, Mr. Grimshaw."

"And I must ask you to accompany us to our Bradburn headquarters."

She put on a coat and scarf without demur.

"At least, that will be a new experience," she said.

The trio walked together down the Upper Crudshaw's central open space, Grimshaw doing his best to make it look to goggling bystanders as if they were taking an amiable stroll after a casual meeting.

"Hullo. Hullo. Hullo! That footgear looks familiar."

A bluff and heavy middle-aged man crossed the Market Place and pointed to the dual-coloured Wellingtons that Grimshaw was carrying.

"I seem to have seen something very similar to those before. On my own premises."

"But not this pair," Millicent Millicheap said with surprising acidity.

"I must say, I'd be surprised if—"

But then Two-faced Tom Barraclough decided not to finish what he had been going to say. These senior policemen, both of whom he knew, undoubtedly knew what they were doing. It was best to leave them to it.

Though everyone in town called him Two-faced, the electorate had voted Barraclough into the council chamber with a heavy majority for years. No one believed his catch-phrase boast that any penny of profit he had ever made had been incidental to the public good yet they continued to maintain him in a position in which his penny profits soared. The man who could look after Thomas Barraclough as Thomas Barraclough did, was no bad bet to look after Upper Crudshaw.

"I'm glad I ran into you two gentlemen," he said. "If you could spare a few minutes—"

Grimshaw looked uncertain. He did not want to keep Millicent Millicheap hanging about in the open view for longer than was necessary. Barraclough caught his hesitation.

"I'm serious about this. I'd like you to come and take a peep in the cellars of our council offices. I won't say more than that. It wouldn't be fair to prejudice you."

"How long do you think—?"

"Five minutes."

"Will you go with Councillor Barraclough, Marsters? I'll sit in the car with Miss Millicheap."

No sooner were they in the caretaker's cubby-hole than Marsters's practised eye went to a large wholesale carton of cigarettes. He at once ran his practised thumb down the sealing-tape and took note of the serial number printed there. Horace Kettle stood in the background, resenting the liberty.

"I bought those from a fellow in the trade."

"Aye, but what trade?"

Kettle knew at once that he was up against someone other than Mosley this time.

And then Marsters's nostrils flared like those of the prophet's warhorse. Nothing is so evocative of a once familar environment as a smell, and if there was one smell that Marsters was competent to recognize, it was the smell of sheep. He went in a die-straight line to a small side-store in which Horace kept such accessories of his trade as replacement broom-handles, cans of Jeyes fluid and floor-sealing compound. And there he found a hessian bale.

"A knife, Kettle."

"That thing's not mine, mister."

"A knife."

Kettle produced something with a blade. Marsters slashed at the stitches. Wool bulged out of the sacking.

"I can explain this," Horace Kettle said.

"I'm sure you can."

Kettle—whom Marsters did not know—looked like a man regularly accustomed to indignant self-exoneration.

"I have reason to believe that this is stolen property."

"It isn't. Honest it isn't. I'll swear on the Good Book. I'm only keeping it here for a mate of yours."

"A mate of mine?"

"Inspector Mosley."

"I think you'd better come with me to Bradburn. We have room in the car for another."

"You ask Inspector Mosley—"

"I can't. He's in Spain."

"It had to do with Reuben Tunnicliffe. Mr. Mosley said—"

"All right. We'll get it all down on paper in due course."

Chapter Nine

After some fifty years of more or less continuous infringement of man's lesser laws, military and civil, it was the first time that Horace Kettle had found himself in trouble—he called it *lumber*—that he saw no way out of. It was the first time he had come up against a slab of humanity quite as unamenable as Marsters: he had usually been able to find some ultimate way round the most inflexible of the RSMs and lieutenant-colonels he had had to accommodate. It was the first time, too, that he had seen Mosley figuring as less than kingpin of the area. As Marsters thundered at him across the interrogation table, Kettle began to see the possibility that this trouble was not going to go away, even when Mosley came home again. There did not seem to him to be enough *esprit de corps* in Marsters's attitude to Mosley.

"I don't want to hear that name on your lips again, Kettle."

"Sir, all I can say is—"

As far as the wholesale cigarettes were concerned, there was nothing that was worth his saying. They belonged to a lost consignment of which the details were held on record in the Bradburn station. He would be formally charged on that account, Marsters said, in midprocess of menacing him, bullying him and trying to trick out of him the name of the fellow he knew who was in the trade.

But when it came to the fleece, Marsters was getting nowhere. Horace Kettle stuck self-righteously to the truth. The bale had been delivered to him as Mosley had said it would. He had looked after it as Mosley had asked him to. He had had no difficulty in finding out from the lorry-driver that it had been despatched by old Nelson Brindley up on Butcher's Brow. Marsters sent a man up Butcher's Brow to get at the facts. Nelson Brindley, after a great deal of circumlocution, confirmed them. Why should Mosley buy a fleece from a one-eyed hill-farmer? There was nothing wrong,

54

the one-eyed farmer argued, with buying and selling fleeces. Folk used them to make bedside rugs. Arty-crafty purists had old-fashioned spinning wheels and spun their own yarn. Mosley had said he wanted a fleece as a present for his niece. He had arranged to store it in the council offices until her birthday. Why should he want to do that? Nelson Brindley was buggered if he knew.

And it all had something to do with Reuben Tunnicliffe, Horace Kettle insisted.

"How can Reuben Tunnicliffe come into it? He's dead."

Horace Kettle did not know. But Mosley had also said that some other man might possibly approach him, perhaps uttering threats. In that case, Kettle's orders were to contact Mosley without delay.

There was only one conclusion that Marsters could come to. The matter of the fleece would have to be shelved until Mosley returned. He himself favoured recalling Mosley immediately, but Grimshaw, in one of his wetter spells, would not hear of interfering with a man's leave. Marsters charged Kettle with unlawful possession of tho cigarettes and the case was put down for hearing in about three weeks' time.

While Marsters was processing Kettle, Grimshaw was treating Millicent Millicheap with detached courtesy. The Assistant Chief Constable had gone pale with consternation at the suggestion that the case must be made over lock, stock and barrel to Special Branch, but when compelled by an unusually forceful Grimshaw to give a firm ruling, he was forced to agree that there did not seem to be any other course.

Nobody liked having Special Branch, MI5 or any other cloak and dagger merchants about a police station. They had a habit of using their essential secrecy as both sword and buckler, as armour-plating and fire-power simultaneously. They came from a distance and derived superiority from the classical remoteness that that bestowed on them. They were only nominally accountable to Chief Constables, and when it came to pulling rank, they could refer back to faceless masterminds who had the ear of people like Prime Ministers. Moreover, they usually had the advantage of a classical education. (The Chief was the only public school man in the Bradburn station, and he had not even made it as far as matriculation.) They had superior private interests (such as collecting snuff-boxes and playing three-dimensional chess) which they wielded to reflect their suavely suppressed contempt for provincial wallies. And one was never free from the suspicion that their eyes were wandering over things that did not concern them—and that they could not possibly understand—little imperfections in the procedures of small forces. Finally, they were likely to make impractical demands, often in the middle of the night, for immediate action for which there existed neither the manpower nor the technology.

Wickham-Skeith, the man they sent over hot-foot from London to treat with Millicent Millicheap was young, tall, lean and dressed as for commuting to a City bank. In his own world he was famed for the number of pseudonyms under which he regularly won, to the point of apparent monopoly, the literary competitions set by intellectual periodicals.

He was sent straight up to the Chief on arrival, and during the preliminary knock-up conversation of gentlemen to whom business must appear to take second place, managed to broach the novels of Harriet Martineau and the abiding influence of Gerard Manley Hopkins, two names that the Chief checked with Central Criminal Records as soon as he was left alone again.

Millicent Millicheap had said that she proposed to derive all the pleasure and interest she could from her first experience of helping the police in their enquiries, and she set about this with fervour, reading every notice on every wall, interpreting with sympathy the features on posters for *Wanted* rapists and taking note of the finer points of kerb-drill. She prattled away to the uniformed constable who was guarding her in the interview room, under strict injunction not to speak a syllable to her.

By five that afternoon, Grimshaw was able to turn for the first time to the stack of near-insolubles that had been accumulating on his desk since nine o'clock: another *Sudden Death* file, whose grieving relict was crying out for a coroner's inquest; a complaint against a detective-sergeant in

P Division that looked as if it might be going to stick; an epidemic of gastro-enteritis in Q that was going to leave the night-shift dangerously undermanned.

A disinterested observer might find faults in Marsters and Grimshaw. They were imperfect men—on the one hand, an officer who was, one might say, a trifle impulsive, disinclined to tolerate minds dissimilar to his own; and in the other corner a struggler unpredictably unsure of himself, perhaps over-concerned at times with considerations of status, forever treading a conscience-pricking path between his natural kindliness and the need to make effective decisions from time to time. But they were both good coppers. Neither was bent. If now and then either of them did a man an injustice, it was not in order to get at that man; it was because they sincerely believed they were right about him. Both of them were meticulous about detail. Each was prepared to work till he dropped—and to carry on from the prone position for as long thereafter as he remained conscious.

When Marsters had finished the laborious paperwork that the channels of justice required for Horace Kettle, he studied interim reports about the state of play of two cases that his sergeants had in hand, then applied his mind to the man who had conned Annie Tunnicliffe. This character's *modus operandi*, together with Annie Tunnicliffe's recognition of him in the album (which Marsters did not accept without qualification) pointed almost certainly at Willy Barber. This probability was reinforced when vehicle registration records came up with the owner of the ancient Cortina whose number-plates Susan Tunnicliffe had noted.

Willy Barber: he appeared to operate under any name that occured to him on the spur of the moment, but Barber was the original brand-label. He had indulged in a similar sort of ploy at Blackpool in the 1960s, another at Whitley Bay in 1972. Always the gentlemen, always ex-colonial, always an offer of marriage with an honourable debt to be settled first. Of course, one did not know what other systems he had worked without winding up inside. The difficulty was knowing where Barber was likely to be at this moment, and what he might be calling himself for the duration of his current bread-earning activity. Barber had a preference for Lancashire and Yorkshire, and Marsters had colleagues in surrounding forces whom he would expect to know if Barber was living on their patch. He did a round of telephoning and got a promising return from Leeds.

After that he perused a few of his sergeants' expense-claims, struck items out of every one of them, then rang for the Weatherline forecast: tonight he had to be out on the moors again. The livestock lorry that Mosley had watched in the gravel-pit had been reported in the neighbourhood again.

While all this was happening, Wickham-Skeith and Millicent Millicheap seemed to be getting on excellently. The young man from Special Branch had lunch sent up to them from the canteen, and the wally who brought it to them reported that they were discussing Ezra Pound.

They went on talking for the whole of the afternoon, then Wickham-Skeith went up to see the Chief—without even clearing it with the Chief's secretary first. The result was that Millicent Millicheap was taken home.

"He's playing it close to his chest," the Assistant Chief Constable said to Grimshaw. "We are to take no further action at all. We are not to approach Miss Millicheap. We are not to try to find the man from the Early Warning Station. Wickham-Skeith did not say so in so many words, but even if she commits an indictable crime, we are to ignore it. I suppose we ought to be grateful to have something taken off our hands, but I fear that Mosley's palatinate is going to be crawling with operators, counter-operators and counter-counter-operators for the foreseeable future. And I must say that Wickham-Skeith is one of nature's optimists. He told the Chief he doubts whether we can hope for any real enlightenment until Mosley gets back. Enlightenment and Mosley in the same breath? In my less responsible moments, I feel a certain zest for a tactical battle between Mosley and Special Branch."

The ACC rang for someone from his outer office to fetch him a packet of cigarettes.

"Incidentally, I've had another caller from Upper Crudshaw —an old girl called Miss Scratby who appears to be a sort of Dalesman's one-woman Festival of Light. She claims that the vicar's wife is running the vicarage as a disorderly house, patronized among others by the Rugger Club. I suppose you'd better send Marsters up to take a quick look. We can't have it said that we do nothing about complaints from the public. And at least, we can be reasonably confident that Mosley isn't behind that, too."

Chapter Ten

Chief Inspector Marsters was an intolerant man, though when it came to working to the book, a predictable one. On occasion he could be moderately shrewd, his tactical potential approximating to that of a chess-player who can sometimes see two moves ahead, but never three. He was never subtle, and was incapable of appreciating subtleties in others.

After half a night in the squalls and bluster of the fells—during which time no rustlers materialized within miles of his ambush, and the suspect sheep-transporter seemed to have vanished from Earth's surface—he tested one of his better-class informants about what was being currently thought and said about the Upper Crudshaw vicarage. He did not believe what his informant told him, his imagination falling short of such flights. How could a couple adore each other, as the Weskitts were said to do, and yet differ doctrinally on their fundamental reason for living in a vicarage? Marsters could not grasp that a couple who differed doctrinally could sincerely be in love: not as Marsters understood love. If it was true that Mrs. Weskitt was a cynical disbeliever, then their marriage must be nearer to the rocks than either of them was prepared to give out; or else it was no more than a lust-match. Total agreement was for Marsters the prerequisite of any successful partnership. Gloria Marsters had not disagreed with an opinion of her husband's for many years; she had decided that she lost nothing by passive concord, and found life quieter that way. It was possible, of course, that Wilfred Weskitt was himself a disbeliever, feigning good churchmanship only for the sake of his stipend and the roof over their heads. The more Marsters thought about it, the more did he incline to that view. For how could a man who held the political opinions expressed from Weskitt's pulpit possibly be a prop of the establishment?

Marsters's tactical sense, however, went so far as not

entering the vicarage in a spirit of frontal attack. He went in on a shallow pretext with, he prided himself, his eyes and ears open.

"One hears some curious rumours in Upper Crudshaw," he said to Cindy Weskitt, "about the suicide of a man called Tunnicliffe. In the hope of hearing something sensible for a change, I'd have liked a word with your husband about it."

But the Reverend Weskitt was not at home. He had been sent for again by the archdeacon, this time to account for the alleged popery embroidered into an altar hanging that he had introduced.

Cindy Weskitt also had tactical acumen. She had weighed Marsters up in a matter of seconds—from his face, his voice, his bearing, and the feudal manner in which he treated his sergeant. Like Mrs. Marsters, she saw the prudence of suppressing her opinions, at least for the time being. She even suppressed, as far as she was able, her ebullient sexy playfulness—though not enough to fool Marsters, who was quick to draw indelible conclusions from her frayed jeans, the contours of her blouse, her loose hair-style and her red-blooded lips. Whoever heard of a vicar's wife in jeans? Marsters also took a sidewise glance to inform himself of the effect that she was having on Sergeant Beamish, who was quite likely to fall blindly for her wiles. But Beamish was not even looking at her. His eye was travelling over Weskitt's bookshelves, at which Marsters also took a passing look: Freud, Orwell—Turgenev, Gorky, Gogol—bloody Bolsheviks. And in full view of any Mothers' Union caller, *The Joy of Sex*. There was a reproduction Beardsley on one wall and a hideous starveling black nude on another who was supposed to represent a hungry Ethiopian Madonna. How could the man have the effrontery to house alongside that a *prie-dieu* with a book-marked Bible open on it, as if to suggest that he daily or nightly knelt there?

"I've heard nothing myself," Cindy Weskitt said. "At least, not at first-hand. But people do say silly things, especially in a place like this, where nothing much ever happens."

"Then might I ask you what you've heard secondhand?" Marsters asked her, in the nearest he could achieve to a silky tone.

She raised her shoulders in general disclaimer. Marsters had heard of young people who buried their jeans in the garden overnight to give them a socially acceptable patina of decay. God knew where this woman had matured hers.

"I've heard nothing that could be of value to a policeman," she said. "Reuben Tunnicliffe was well known and well liked. By hanging himself he set up a shock-wave. There was bound to be speculation—and it was bound to be ill informed."

She was the only one drawn into the case so far who did not plead any connection with Mosley: she could see as many moves ahead in the game as that.

Marsters came away with the feeling that his visit had not been entirely wasted. He had confirmed that Upper Crudshaw had a vicar who, to judge from his library, was dominated by radical secularities, was obsessed by erotica and had a wife who could not be anything but an embarrassment to him in his parish rounds. Marsters did admit to himself, however, that all this did fall short of proving the vicarage was used as a brothel. Marsters did not really believe that the vicarage was used as brothel. A life spent close to crime, some of it monstrous, had done nothing to stimulate his sluggish imagination. But smoke only came from fire, and something indiscreet might perhaps have been allowed to happen. It was too early yet to dismiss the allegation out of hand: women who denounced their neighbours on moral grounds rarely gave up easily. Marsters would leave Beamish behind to do some discreet surveillance in the town. He took the sergeant round a corner into an unfrequented back-street and briefed him about the surveillance that he wanted done, with a plethora of detail about how to set about it.

Marsters had not wanted Beamish on the case. He did not like Beamish. Beamish had a reputation for thinking that he knew it all, and could do it all single-handed. Moreover, Beamish had been put to work on more than one case with Mosley, and they had ended up as friends, which was enough to damn the chances of any up-and-coming youngster. To Marsters it was the height of insanity to put a friend of Mosley's on the track of a history in which Mosley had clearly been acting like an imbecile: perhaps that was the reason Grimshaw had insisted on it—another testimony to Grimshaw's wetness. He seemed to look on Beamish as an interpreter of Mosley.

But Beamish had mellowed since his early promotion in the CID, under the influence partly of Mosley, and partly of an outrageously off-beam social worker whom he was said to be seriously courting up Marldale way. Like Cindy Weskitt, he saw the dangers of rubbing Marsters up the wrong way. But here one could only do one's best: the friction might all be coming from Marsters.

"A low profile, that's what you're going to need. Have you ever kept a low profile in your life, Beamish?"

"I think I can claim that, sir—where it has seemed appropriate."

"Well, it's appropriate here and now, Beamish, make no mistake about that. They don't know you in Upper Crudshaw, I take it?"

"They'll have seen me with you, sir," Beamish said.

Marsters looked at him sharply, uncertain whether that was meant as insolence.

"A lot of the people who are seen with me end up behind bars, Sergeant Beamish."

Marsters went back to his car and raised HQ on his radio to ask about developments in any of his other current interests. The sheep-transporter had been seen again, having lagered up for the night in a lane behind a copse. It had not transported any sheep, but a belated report had come in of thefts from the flock of a farmer called Brindley whom even the constable on the switchboard referred to as Nelson. But that was only the wonder of a moment. Leeds had come up with a positive location of Willy Barber. He was being watched, but was not at the moment committing any discernible offence. Should Marsters ask them to hold him, or should he persuade Grimshaw to get the necessary clearance, so he could go in himself? He decided on the latter: Marsters was a great one for doing things himself, if they were to be done properly.

As soon as the chief inspector had left Upper Crudshaw, Beamish—even the highly self-organized Beamish—was conscious of relief from oppression. It was like the removal of a burden, except that his shoulders did not feel about to rise in flight. He let them sag. Beamish had the knack of transforming himself from a smart young detective to a hobbledehoy-about-town without needing any change of clothes. He could think himself into roles. He let his shoulders droop, began breathing through a dejected mouth. His eyes seemed to film over behind a cloud of feeble intellect. He went and drank a plastic mug of sludgy coffee in Upper Crudshaw's least enticing café, lost his change in the fruit-machine there, and emerged to shuffle seedily about what a dead-beat yobbo might find to look at in the town.

It was in the telephone kiosk that he made his first discovery: graffiti.

LADIES—DO YOU NEED A HEAVY-BREATHER? FOR THIS AND OTHER SERVICES RING CRUDSHAW 489.

Could that possibly be the number of the vicarage? He looked in the directory, and the Weskitts' was a six-digit number. So he rang Bradburn Station to have 489 traced for him.

It turned out to belong to Messrs. Aitken, Henderson and Brigg, Solicitors. He strolled past their window, looked in and saw Teddy Bemrose pontificating to some old dear about her rent-book.

Chapter Eleven

Willy Barber shampooed his creamy white hair every night and had it cut every three weeks, short back and sides. He was pleasantly spoken in the precise fashion of the educated Lancashire man who respects the English language, and was a throwback to the type of gentleman once defined as one who could never willingly hurt another's feelings. This was not a mere character-pretence on Barber's part. It was either his natural disposition, or else he had projected himself thus for so many years that his gentlemanliness had become a permanency. It was the second strongest weapon in his armoury; his first was his unadulterated natural talent for dishonesty. He even succeeded in maintaining his slightly remote aplomb throughout the ordeal of interview by Chief Inspector Marsters, his only adverse reaction being a faint suggestion of personal hurt that anyone should make such accusations against him.

Marsters was using one of his favourite techniques. He roared his charges across the table, his lips sometimes within inches of Barber's ear. Then, when Barber denied them with quiet emphasis, he behaved as if what he had just heard was a confession. It did not matter what words Barber had used: Marsters pretended to have heard something else. There was perhaps no need for any of this. Annie Tunnicliffe's complaint was well backed up by the evidence of her daughter and Barber had done time more than once for offences identical in structure. But a confession, with court-time saved by a *Guilty* plea and an ample *taken into consideration* sheet into the bargain, was always a tidy way of rounding a case off.

It took half an hour for Barber to give in, and then it was in a suave manner, with the innuendo that he was only doing so to put an end to the exhibition of near-insanity that was going on opposite him.

"But I wouldn't be too certain of a conviction, Chief Inspector. I had told the woman I wanted to marry her,

and I would have come back and done so, once I had got
this little debt of honour out of the way. I can't sleep at
night with debts of honour on my mind, Chief Inspector."

Marsters produced a combination of snort and gulp that
seemed to emanate from a fatal failure of his vocal organs.

"She should have waited a little longer for me, Mr. Marsters. That's what my solicitor will say. To my mind it was
the daughter who sent her rushing after you people. You
wait till the good lady sees me again. She'll be the first to
declare it was all a misunderstanding."

"There was no misunderstanding about your leaving her
a false address."

"On that point, I reserve my defence."

Marsters became quiet, and set about the paperwork.

In his tour of the curiosities of the town, Beamish stopped
to examine the hand-written notices in the glass panels of
a stationer's door. An offer to exchange a two-stroke mo-
torcycle for budgerigars was matched by a man who had
for sale a twin-seater baby-buggy, a home-brewing kit and
a goat, which he would sell outright or trade for missing
numbers in his sets of 1930s cigarette-cards: *Cries of London* preferred. There were no direct offers of French lessons
or relief from tension at the hands of a Swedish masseuse,
but Beamish's eye homed in on a familiar telephone number.

FOR TOMORROW'S WINNERS, RING CRUDSHAW 489.

It really did look as if the town's leading solicitors were
diversifying.

Beamish rang Upper Crudshaw 489 and was answered
by a clipped elderly voice that invited him to state his
business.

"I'm ringing about an advertisement that I saw in a telephone booth," Beamish said.

There was a long pause. Then the desiccated voice said,
"Ah," then paused again.

"Perhaps we could make an appointment?" Beamish suggested.

"I am sorry I am not able to help you," came at last.

"But the advertisement said—"

"I am only too well aware what the advertisement says,

but I am afraid that I cannot be of assistance. The gentleman who conducts this aspect of our affairs is away on holiday. Perhaps if you were to ring again after the nineteenth of the month—"

That was the day after Mosley was due back.

"How disappointing."

When he came home from his latest round with the archdeacon, the Reverend Wilfred Weskitt was more weary and frustrated than his wife ever remembered having seen him. It had been the most merciless attack to which he had ever had to submit. Yet this was one occasion on which he was as blameless as a baby. It was only from a middle pew, and by a parishioner with failing eyesight, that the embroidered arabesques on the fringes of his new altar-cloth could possibly be mistaken for an idolatrous row of saints' profiles.

"Quite beside the point," the archdeacon said. "If you were to conduct yourself in an orthodox fashion in other respects, blind old people in middle pews would not be scrounging round for brickbats to throw at you. And don't tell me that the woman told you to do it, Weskitt. It was up to Adam to control the creature God had fashioned for him."

Cindy did not judge this a felicitous moment to tell her husband that she had had a visit from the scuffers.

At half past five, when Teddy Bemrose had finished for the day, he locked up Aitken, Henderson and Brigg's offices and, looking for all the world like a stick-insect, walked up to the Market Place where he had parked his Ford Prefect. On his way he had to pass the telephone-booth in which Beamish had noted the graffiti. Ever since that notice had appeared, Teddy Bemrose had been unable to pass that kiosk without averting his eyes. It was true that he had not written the lines himself, but he knew more than a solicitor's managing clerk ought to have done about how they came to be there.

Beamish and Deirdre Harrison spent an evening together in Upper Crudshaw. Deirdre was the young social worker from the Marldale area who was believed by some to be

having an influence on him. It was also visible to her friends
that he was exercising influence on her. She was a large,
unwieldy girl, who wore her clothes as if they had blown
themsleves on to her in a fell-top gale. Her language could
have produced awed silence on a herring wharf. She insisted
on being addressed as Ms., and her contempt for the social
services rule book was equalled by her consummate knowledge of every small-print clause in it that could be pulled
to support her purpose of the moment.

Now she had reverted to calling herself Miss. In conversation with Beamish she now used obscenities only in
verbatim quotations. She wore clothes that though admit-
tedly not in fashion, were recognizably feminine—and she
occasionally stopped talking for Beamish himself to do so.
Beamish, for his part, was taking pains to show that he was
not as stodgy as some men said he was. He made attempts
from time to time—sometimes pathetically off-target—to
prove himself capable of frivolity. And he and Deirdre met
two or three times a week, their duty and emergency calls
permitting.

Tonight they chose the Hanging Gate, Upper Crudshaw's
fifteenth-century coaching inn, whose dining-room spe-
cialized in undeniably English cooking, in whose classless
public bar pigeon-fanciers rubbed shoulders with the own-
ers of racing whippets and in whose sporting-printed lounge
the respectable occasional drinkers of Crudshaw occasionally drank.

Beamish piloted Deirdre to a table as far away from any
other as could be managed and began to tell her in a low
voice how he had passed his day. He had no conscience
about talking to her about matters that were strictly not for
non-police ears. Deirdre was different. She was absolutely
safe. She knew and greatly liked Mosley, and the three of
them together had once shared the devious strategy of a
characteristic Mosley case. The confidentiality that that had
engendered had continued as a natural course.

She laughed when she heard of the caching of a fleece
in Horace Kettle's store-cellar. She laughed immoderately
at the allegations made about the vicarage—Deirdre Harrison laughing immoderately involved an output of decibels
that temporarily silenced conversation in other corners of

the bar, and indeed in other rooms in the inn, including the one upstairs in which the Rugger Buggers were conducting the loose scrum that was their monthly business meeting.

But Beamish did not tell her about the Millicheap Connection. The shadow of Special Branch affected even personal relationships.

"It makes one wonder what the old monkey's up to now," Beamish said.

"I would have thought it was pretty obvious what he's up to."

"It's not obvious to anyone in my working environment."

"Surely he believes that this man Tunnicliffe was being small-time blackmailed, and so he has scattered Upper Crudshaw with other temptations for a small-time blackmailer."

"That had, of course, occurred to me."

"You know it bloody well hadn't," Deirdre Harrison said.

It was at this moment that a young lady of evidently formidable intentions got up from the table at which she was sitting with a man and came over to Beamish and Deirdre. Like Deirdre, she was not one who expended much thought, effort or money on her appearance. Her hair was long and lifeless, her sweater could have been worn with grace by a substantially bigger woman and her skirt, faintly reminiscent of a hunting tartan, had survived a more colourful past. She appeared to be very angry about something.

"I wouldn't like you to think that I make a habit of eavesdropping, but when one hears one's own name being bandied about—"

"I'm sorry," Beamish said. "But if one might ask what one's own name is—?"

"Tunnicliffe."

She fired the syllables at him without properly opening her teeth. It was difficult to know whether she hated her surname, or whether she was thrusting it at him as a challenge.

"There are any number of Tunnicliffes in this part of the country," Beamish said.

"That's as may be. Another name I heard you say in the same context was Mosley."

"I'm not aware that pronouncing the word Mosley is an offence against anyone."

"It's an offence against me—in a public place."

"I'm sorry—"

Beamish was genuinely bewildered as to where his offence lay.

"I suppose," she said, "that you two belong to Mosley's lot."

"I'm off duty at the moment, but it is true that I have worked from time to time with a man called Mosley—if it's the same Mosley that you're thinking of."

"Of course it is. You know very well it is. Listen—my name is Susan Tunnicliffe. You know what happened to my father—while the balance of his mind was disturbed, as they used to put it in their comforting way. I think we have suffered enough, my mother and I. I don't propose to stand for any more harassment."

"I'm quite sure, Miss Tunnicliffe, that you have no call—"

"It is harassment to have our affairs discussed freely in an inn, in such a way as to make the public at large think that something has not been as it should be. Now will you be so kind as to tell me who you are and from what station you operate?"

"I see no harm in telling you that."

Beamish gave her that information, which she received as if she found it very distasteful indeed.

"And this young woman?"

She looked at Deirdre with repugnance. Deirdre had already disciplined herself to stay out of this.

"This young *lady*—"

Beamish had not missed the tone of *woman*.

"This young lady is a friend of mine. She is not a member of the police force."

"I see."

Susan Tunnicliffe tightened bloodless lips.

"I see. In that case, I will certainly put in a complaint. That you should sit here, discussing with an outsider idle speculation heard in the course of duty—"

"You are making an unnecessary fuss about nothing whatever."

"We shall see."

She went back to the man she was with, a curly-headed, frighteningly well-built specimen of the type who starts putting on fat at the age when he starts making less regular use of his muscle. He was Irish, a peripatetic foreman on building sites up and down the Greater Manchester area.

"What do you think's got into her?" Deirdre asked.

"Over-wrought by all that's happened. I'm not worried."

"I should bloody well think not. Let's go somewhere else. I always feel safer in public bars than in the haunts of the bourgeoisie."

Beamish's eyes narrowed. Deirdre knew that he was doing mental arithmetic. When he had to drive, he had a formula by which he kept track of his bloodstream alcohol: 17 milligrammes per millilitre for every half pint of bitter, minus 15 milligrammes an hour burnt up by his metabolism.

"There's no need for all that," Deirdre had told him more than once. "Two and a half pints are the limit, and for a man in your position, two's the safe ceiling. Up to now you've had a pint and a half."

They crossed the road to the unpresumptuously named Dog, in whose public bar any group which tried to separate itself from the main gathering was suspect. The drinkers in the Dog were an integrated community. It was in every sense a *public* house, and what one got out of the company depended on what one contributed.

At the moment of their entry, the congregation was discussing the "short, sharp shock" treatment of juvenile offenders. A shaven-scalped, barrel-chested fifty-year-old was very strongly in favour of it.

"Did you ever have a short, sharp shock in your life?" Deirdre asked him.

"My life has been one long, sharp shock, ducky."

They had been in there about twenty minutes when two breath-taking strangers came in. It had to be a breath-taking arrival to halt a debate in the Dog.

These two were tarts. Not Upper Crudshaw tarts. Not tarts of a calibre that one could ever picture operating in Upper Crudshaw; tarts who would have drawn attention to their tartiness even in the most sinful corners of Bradburn.

They were almost but not quite punk-cult figures: hair in a spiky tightness that drew attention to the barely credible smallness of their skulls. But their hair was not dyed in unmentionable colours: one was raven-black, the other had the makings of a Nashville Goldilocks. One was in black leather, including a mini-skirt that looked as if it would split if she attempted a pace of more than nine inches. The other wore a flared trouser-suit with a collar that hung to where her belly-button was and had had a distant origin in naval rig. Both were made up with their eyes beaded down in deep black sockets. Both looked as if their faces would crack like the glaze of over-heated porcelain if they were to risk a smile.

The silence into which they shocked the Dog lasted for long seconds. When the conversation resumed, it was relatively subdued.

"What about a kitty for a few short, sharp shocks there, Tommy?"

The newcomers asked for Bacardi *and* rum. With his Dalesman's urbanity, the landlord served them without comment. Then one of them asked if he could direct them to the vicarage.

When he received Susan Tunnicliffe's complaint, Marsters's reaction was not what some might have predicted. It was true that he did not like Beamish, but he liked complaining civilians even less—especially those who claimed engagement in artistry of any kind.

He had Beamish in.

"Just tell me, lad, what happened in the Crudshaw Hanging Gate."

The intonation of the *lad* told Beamish that if he played this cannily—and with a modicum of luck—he might get away with it.

"Why, Beamish, were you talking about Mosley and the Tunnicliffes at all? They weren't in your brief. I sent you to Upper Crudshaw to nose the ground for rumours about the vicarage."

"Sir, it's impossible to assess anything in Upper Crudshaw without running into Mosley's tracks."

Marsters's eyes ignited.

"You've come across Mosley's name in connection with the vicarage?"

"No, sir—not exactly."

"What the hell is *not exactly* supposed to mean? Either you have or you haven't."

"I haven't, sir."

He had decided to say nothing to Marsters, for the time being at any rate, about the small-time blackmail theory. He wanted to take a closer walk round it himself—and preferably wait till he could have a word with Mosley. It would not be all that long now.

"And this girl you were talking to?"

"A very reliable informant, sir. I was using her as my cover for being in Upper Crudshaw at all."

Marsters grunted.

"Well, it seems to me you've run out of plausible cover for any more hanging about up there. You have compromised yourself good and proper. I'm moving you on to somewhere else. You are a young man with his name to make. There is one sure and certain way in which a man could make his name in these hills at this moment in time, Beamish—and that has to do with sheep. I have a file here about sheep that I'd like you to apply your mind to."

Helmeted men trying shop-door handles, detective-constables on pickpocket duty at Cowburn point-to-point races, report-writing sergeants searching for elusive letters on typewriter keyboards—they still came out occasionally into broad smiles that had nothing to do with their task of the moment. They had just suddenly remembered their own favourite image of *All White Jack* on the Costa del Sol.

But *All White* Mosley's beach-life was no longer considered a permissible jest in higher circles.

"What are we going to do about him, Tom?" the Assistant Chief Constable wanted to know. "Confront him? Suspend him?"

"What does the Chief say?"

"That he doesn't feel he ought to interfere with the way I run my department."

"He must have given you some idea of which way his mind is working."

Grimshaw resisted the obvious temptation. Or perhaps he was too weary to think of it.

"He did say it's a pity we can't extend Mosley's leave. But I don't take that seriously. We have no precedent, and it would certainly create one. And I have an idea that Mosley's probably had his fill of Spain by now."

"What do Special Branch have to suggest?"

The ACC looked relieved. He was always openly grateful for constructive help. He picked up his phone, and after several interrupted connections, was eventually talking to Wickham-Skeith.

"Yes—Yes—Yes, indeed—No, indeed—No, indeed—Yes, indeed—"

He put the phone back in its cradle.

"We're to do nothing at all, Tom. What was decided about Millicent Millicheap and the Early Warning Mole applies equally to Mosley. It's a favourite mode of action with the Security people. They behave as if they haven't a clue what's going on. They interfere with nobody. They let things develop, see who contacts whom, watch how communications are carried. As Wickham-Skeith put it, they don't like breaking bits off the edges. They wait until they have enough leverage to lift the whole lid. So we are to give Mosley as much latitude of movement as we consider compatible with efficiency."

Grimshaw gave a laugh that he did his best to make into a hollow one.

"Mosley—latitude—since when did we ever have to give him any? What's going to happen if he gets the message that all the brakes are off? Mosley is going to be watched —his every move, Wickham-Skeith assured me, his every utterance and his every contact. Mosley is until further notice the concern of higher beings than us. I'm not quite sure where I'd put my money if I were a betting man."

Chapter Twelve

It was remarkable with what range of ingenuity all ranks found pretexts to linger in or near Bradburn station on the morning of Mosley's return from his Mediterranean sortie.

655 PC Harburn, who had actually once been seen off on his beat, came in again because he claimed that he had been taken short—and who could challenge the functional needs of a constable's inner man? One of the panda cars, despatched on a routine patrol of the northern bypass, had reversed and parked in an entry not fifty yards from HQ, ostensibly to keep tabs on a suspected loiterer with intent, more obviously in the hope of seeing Mosley arrive.

Their colleagues in Panda Two were still in the yard, had the bonnet of their vehicle up and were going through the motions of locating a blown fuse. In the CID Room two detective-constables were doing a painfully slow boxsearch of a street-map that they could have drawn from memory.

Even in higher places there were readable symptoms of half-hearted application. Detective-Superintendent Grimshaw was working with his door ajar, his concentration dissipated from time to time as his ears fancied they detected excitement below stairs. Farther along the corridor the Assistant Chief Constable was finding it difficult to follow the argument of the *Daily Telegraph* leader—he considered it reasonable for a senior man to bone up on the wider world in official time.

By ten minutes past the hour Mosley had still not arrived. At twelve minutes past the two detectives were within an ace of folding up their map. And then at a quarter past, two positive things happened. The duty station-sergeant suddenly noticed how many people were cluttering up his front office, queuing up to ask for items of information which any one of them could have furnished by reflex action. Station-Sergeant Halfhide raised his eyes from a report of Saturday's match at Shenfield Road and cleared the room with the sort of roar that Mosley, if he had still been there, might have heard in the streets of Pamplona. More delicately, the ACC dialled Grimshaw's extension.

"Is Jack back, Tom?"

It had beome the convention since the onset of Mosley's latest round of atrocities to eschew all personal elements in speaking of or even, as far as one could, in thinking about him. They had stopped talking about him by his Christian name. It was some measure of the general tension that the ACC's resolve should slip in a single sentence.

"Not as far as I'm aware," Grimshaw said.

"He's late."

This was a highly academic point because, Mosley's area sprawling as it did, it was not common for him to start his day at the hub of law-enforcement. Still, after a fortnight's absence in Andalusia—

"I dare say he'll have gone straight to Upper Crudshaw," Grimshaw said.

"Ought we not to be keeping some sort of track on him?"

"If you remember, sir, our orders were to do nothing about him at all. Just let him shuttle about in his normal way, and leave the tracking to others."

"Yes," the ACC said uncertainly.

"There'll be no lack of vigilance on Mosley. Wherever he sets a foot, other feet will follow."

Grimshaw was revisited by a previous feeling that he might be going to enjoy this. How clever were they, Special Branch, MI5 and whatever other unknown quantities had entered for this paper chase? How long before Mosley spotted what was going on behind him? What monstrous counter-activity would then follow?

"There's not much more, I think, sir, that we can do but wait," he said to the ACC.

Upper Crudshaw was, then, a small town under vital surveillance by Special Branch, MI5 and such sundry other esoteric agencies as felt that the security of the state was threatened by goings-on that they did not understand. It was also obvious—though not perhaps immediately apparent—that anything involving the Early Warning Station on Crudshaw Nab must also attract the attention of the

CIA, the KGB and similar bodies in the pay of any power whose activities were susceptible of Early Warning.

Upper Crudshaw must, then, have been an ant-hill of counter-counter espionage at nine o'clock on the morning of Mosley's return to duty. There should have been men who did not belong to British Telecom, pretending to be doing maintenance at the tops of telegraph poles. There should have been holes in the road, manned by watchers who knew nothing about gas-leaks, fish-lines or sewers. There should have been men leaning on the corners of walls who were not known to the public of Crudshaw.

There was indeed a man at the top of a telegraph pole, but by some strange coincidence he was an accredited British Telecom engineer, attempting to track down a real and many times reported fault. There was indeed a roped off hole in the road, but it had not been manned since it had been pneumatically drilled ten days ago. There was indeed a man leaning with one shoulder against the corner wall of the Hanging Gate, smoking a cigarette for which he had had to pay the shop-counter price: Horace Kettle who was on bail pending summary justice, and under suspension from the municipal boilers pending the formal decision about his guilt.

Upper Crudshaw could not honestly be said to present a decor suggestive of international intrigue. There was as usual a thirty-yard tail-back behind Dicky Edmunds's milk-float in the High Street. One of Two-faced Tom's hod-carriers, in dual-coloured Wellingtons, had slipped up into town to buy a postal order for his pools coupon. A woman with the future of her crowning glory assured by twisted bits of rag was talking to another who had opted for the higher technology of blue plastic rollers. Otherwise Upper Crudshaw could not be said to be busy. Anyone who believed that Upper Crudshaw was under observation by the world's masterspies—and the town's conversation had been about little else for days—must have been convinced that the world's undercover systems were extraordinarily talented at self-concealment.

Then two things happened that turned this into a special day.

First an Austin Princess taxi, on hire from two villages away, slid into the Market Place and its driver asked someone the whereabouts of the address to which he had been called. Five minutes later he was driving out of town again, two women sunk back into his rear seat as if they were not keen on being stared at. They were Annie and Susan Tunnicliffe, on their way to give evidence at Willy Barber's committal proceedings.

Then secondly the single-decker red bus arrived that brought people up from Bradburn and intermediate stages by an intricate series of loops and diversions up and around the valleys.

Out of this bus there climbed the miscellany of passengers who climbed out of it every morning—plus one man who only occasionally came by this means: Mosley, looking, if one studied him hard and imaginatively enough, as if he had caught as much of the sun as had been able to get in under the brim of his homburg.

Mosley stopped to speak to no one and acknowledged only vacantly such tentative greetings as were waved at him. He went straight across to the offices of Messrs. Aitken, Henderson and Brigg.

"Nah, Teddy."

"Good morning, Inspector," Teddy Bemrose said frigidly.

Chief Inspector Marsters gave his evidence of arrest, and of Barber's alleged statement quietly, honestly and unemotionally. When he had finished, the man seemed to stand condemned, further hearing superfluous. Marsters went and sat at the back of the court.

Willy Barber, graciously allowed to sit down in the dock after the clerk had recorded his not guilty plea, looked unharried, confident and prepared to forgive his accusers— all with that combination of patience, charm and addiction to old world standards that had in his time inspired so many impressionable ladies to settle his honourable debts for him.

Annie Tunnicliffe was called, eighty-one years of anything but frailty. She was quietly and neatly costumed, and as confident in her assertions as Marsters had been in his, the blunt simplicity of her local speech adding an uncompromising element. It was clear that Annie Tunnicliffe was here to see Willy Barber go down.

"It was when I found out that there was no such street as the address he gave me—"

And it was at this stage that the suave Mr. Barber forgot points about court procedure with which he must surely have been thoroughly familiar. He stood up in the dock and gripped the front rail.

"Now look here, Annie—please tell it as it was—"

The chairman of the bench was properly outraged, and said all the things that are proper for a chairman to say in face of such a disturbance. Barber would have his full opportunity at the proper moment. Barber's dock-brief rose, turned, and whispered to his client.

Yet Barber persisted.

"Annie—I told you there were things I'm not proud of. I told you were there were things that I had to tidy up. And you said that what was past was over. It was better for us all that left hand should not know too much about right hand. Those were your very words."

The magistrate threatened the accused with exclusion from the remainder of the hearing. Barber replied with a little bow of apologetic respect.

"I am most deeply sorry, sir. I promise I'll not interrupt again. May I have your permission to resume my seat?"

Chief Inspector Marsters was utterly at a loss to understand what followed next. But then he may have been impervious to the charm inherent in Willy Barber's voice. He had not been privileged to form the same associations with Willy Barber's voice as Annie Tunnicliffe had. Marsters had not spent a dirty weekend with Barber at Packer's Hydro, Blackpool North Shore. He had not had sweet nothings whispered in his ear by Barber in cliff shelters up and down the Fylde coast. He had not sat in the spacious luxury of Barber's maroon Cortina, listening to Willy's nostalgia for the lost epoch of self-respect and courtesy between all men. Annie had been in all these situations—and after a lifetime with Reuben, had been impressed by Willy Barber's refinement.

"Well, come to think of it," she said under oath. "I'm not at all sure. It could all have been a misunderstanding."

The prosecuting solicitor did his best to steer her back into line. But even his most persuasive questions could prove no more than that the complainant had irrevocably changed her mind about complaining. Adjournment for consultation. Case withdrawn by leave.

Annie Tunnicliffe and Willy Barber left the court together. Marsters went back to HQ to take it out of Beamish if he had not some convincing excuse for failing to apprehend last night's sheep-thieves.

Beamish was not at HQ. Marsters ought to have known that he would not be. Beamish's time-sheet gave him at least some compensation for a wasted night in the open air.

But Beamish was not at his billet when Marsters, heedless of a sergeant's possible need for daytime sleep, spoke to his landlady on the phone. Beamish had not gone to bed immediately he had got home. For although sheep had unlawfully changed hands during the night, and Beamish had been in the wrong place to intervene, he had had thoughts on the subject. Beamish saw, as he was always seeing—and saying—that his superiors' approach to this crime had been misguided. He saw that nothing was being gained by all this peering into darkness, lonely, cold, wet and bored to the brink of insanity. This was management crime—and it was from the top rather than the bottom that it was going to be broken.

So he started to read the hefty file again, forgetting to eat his breakfast. And then Deirdre rang. She was spending the morning at Stopeley, sitting on a subcommittee to appoint a warden for a new sheltered housing project. If he could manage to get out that way, he could have the pleasure of taking her out for a ploughman's lunch. And she had something startling to tell him about Upper Crudshaw.

Teddy Bemrose was in as disorganized a state as Mosley had ever seen him. Until this moment, if he had been asked to name a man who epitomized all the sterling virtues that some men said were dying, Mosley would have raised his pointer towards old Teddy. The discomfort of the old man's celluloid wing collar spoke of unrelenting self-discipline.

The ancient suit through which his fleshless joints protruded like drumsticks bore witness to his innate austerity in all things. The steady certainty of his pale blue eyes guaranteed a faultless reading of the motivation of all men he met.

Not so this morning. This morning, in Mosley's presence, Teddy Bemrose spoke sharply to an inoffensive old lady who had come in with a standard and legitimate request for her landlord to replace a fallen tile. Behind the cutting edge of his collar, Bemrose's scraggy neck suggested that he denied himself all those things in life that were worth having and resented their enjoyment by others. His dust-impregnated, chair-and-desk-worn herringbone made one wonder how long it would be before he delighted his employers' hearts by speaking tentatively of retirement. And his eyes, filmed with fatigue, refused at first to meet Mosley's. When he did so far remember himself as to raise them, they were hostile and accusing.

"All I can say about what you have started up in Upper Crudshaw, Inspector Mosley, is that you are in this on your own from now on. I will play no further part in it."

"I didn't ask you to play very much part in it," Mosley said. "I only asked you for the loan of your office phone number, and to tell any enquirers to place a two-way bet on the second favourite in any race they enquired about. Have there been any enquiries, by the way?" he asked with boyish eagerness.

"You didn't tell me what indecencies you were going to use a long-established family firm to advertise."

"Indecencies?"

"You also advertised this office as providing by telephone amenities for which I am surprised there is any demand: heavy breathing, for example. I had a caller from as far afield as Preston, asking if our services included coy little whimpers of delight. He expressed himself ready to pay for them in advance, in multiples of three minutes. There has even been an enquirer with the manner of a policeman in every shade of his voice. Which suggests to me that someone has traced this phone number—"

Policeman? Which policeman? Who from the Bradburn

force had been poking his nose into Upper Crudshaw? Mosley felt the first of what was to become an accumulation of qualms.

"A sergeant by the name of Beamish."

Mosley relaxed. He could handle Beamish. Beamish was his friend.

"And what did you tell him?"

"What you told me to tell any obstreperous caller—that the man who handles this sort of thing was away on holiday."

"There's no harm done, then."

"No harm done, Inspector? With Millicent Millicheap taken to Bradburn and held for questioning all day?"

"Beamish took Miss Millicheap in for questioning?"

"Not Sergeant Beamish. Your Chief Inspector Marsters came first. Then the second time, your Detective Superintendent Grimshaw came with him."

"Oh dear."

"Yes—it is *oh dear*, isn't it, Inspector?"

"What could Marsters want to question Miss Millicheap about."

"There is much speculation about that. Lips appear to be very tightly sealed."

"I'd like to know what brought Marsters here in the first place."

"I can tell you that. Two things. One was a carton of stolen cigarettes in the basement of the council offices."

"Ah."

"And a bale of sheep's wool."

"Oh dear."

"Horace Kettle has been charged."

Not good. Mosley saw that this was not good. He saw that things had gone wrong. He was not prepared to admit to Teddy Bemrose at this moment how much seemed to have gone wrong. He had had no fears about leaving a few ploys in midstream while he was away for a fortnight. Upper Crudshaw and some thirty square miles round the place was an area that he sometimes did not have to visit for months at a time. Why should it become a vortex of sinfulness overnight? And had he not asked the vicar's wife to keep a watchful eye on things for him? Had he overestimated her sang-froid?

"And someone played a confidence trick on Annie Tunnicliffe. You didn't put me in the picture about that, Inspector."

"Put you in the picture? That was nothing to do with me, Teddy."

"That makes a change," Bemrose said. "Anyway, they've got the man. Chief Inspector Marsters arrested him. A fellow called Barber."

"That'll be Willy."

Mosley knew him. But he did not let the lawyer's clerk see all that he was thinking and feeling. He ought, of course, to have known that Marsters would need no urging to come prying in Crudshaw.

"I feel as if you've turned me into a criminal," Bemrose said. "Goodness knows what the partners will say, if any of this comes to their ears. Especially that advertisement in the telephone booth. They will have me put away for certain."

"Criminal? You've done nothing criminal, Teddy. I've done nothing criminal. All I have done is to organize a few fruity rumours—with the full permission of all the people concerned. And all in the best of causes."

Which looked as if it was still unsolved—unscratched—untouched. Why had Reuben Tunnicliffe hanged himself?

"And the worst thing of all," Bemrose said, "is the irresponsible story you put out about the vicarage."

"That will all come out in the wash. Be denied. Be disproved. The vicar will be strengthened by the wave of public sympathy. People have a bottomless hatred of unfairness. They might even start going to his church."

"Life will never be normal again, Inspector Mosley. Because I'm afraid that what you started as a rumour has turned out to be true. The vicarage *is* being used for immoral purposes."

In the vicarage, the Reverend Wilfred Weskitt was opening his morning mail. Opposite him across the breakfast-table, his wife was looking as fresh and interesting as does any well-made young woman who is wearing nothing at all under a towelling bath-robe.

There was always the hope that somewhere among the

little stack of envelopes there might be one that contained life-changing news. And this morning there was. But it was not a favourable reply to the Reverend Weskitt's offer to broadcast religious talks. It was not an acceptance by an editor of one of his wholesomely exciting stories for young adults. It was not the offer of a remunerative post by a Missionary Society.

It was in an envelope on which the address looked barely literate. It was printed in ungainly capitals on feint-ruled octavo paper. And the message consisted of a single word:

WHOREMONGER

"I thought you ought to know," Deirdre said, over their ploughman's, "that I've been doing a bit of digging around in Upper Crudshaw."

Beamish considered this legitimate enough. There were various and obvious reasons why she was likely to come across things more easily than he might.

"I'm not so sure after all about our small-time blackmail theory. Though there is, of course, the old adage—that I've never understood—about exceptions proving rules."

"What are you getting at?"

"It seems to me that the Upper Crudshaw vicarage *is* a brothel."

Chapter Thirteen

When Mosley came out of the lawyers' office, Horace Kettle had moved. He had crossed the courtyard archway entrance of the Hanging Gate and it was his left shoulder that was now reinforcing the wall.

"Mr. Mosley—"

Mosley stopped in mid-pace and turned his head.

"You've dropped me right in it, you have."

"I strenuously deny that. I warned you about those cigarettes."

"And that bloody great bale of wool. I told them, you know. I told them how I came to have all that bloody wool down there. I told them it's yours. I had to."

"You'll be in no trouble over the fleece. It's my fleece. I have a receipt for it. Any man can buy a fleece and keep it anywhere he wants. Or have it kept for him."

That, of course, was not the attitude that was going to be taken in some circles with which Mosley was familiar. Mosley was beginning to wonder what had got into him during the run-up to his holiday. It must have been some sort of brain-storm. He must have become childishly excited. He must have thought Spain was a good deal farther away from Upper Crudshaw that it was.

He began to move away from Kettle. Kettle was a minor miscreant who had been living on the brink of minor nemesis for years. He could hardly have hoped to survive an incursion by Marsters down the boiler-room steps.

Kettle took a pace to keep up with Mosley and touched him on the sleeve.

"So what are you going to do for me, Mr. Mosley?"

"There's nothing I can do," Mosley said, more gruffly than he usually spoke to people.

"Oh yes there is, Mr. Mosley. They'll listen to you. They've done nothing about that bale of wool—it's not even on the charge-sheet—yet. They said they wouldn't do anything till you came back and they could ask you about it."

"So I'll tell them about it. But that won't get you off the hook for the cigarettes."

"They'll listen to you, Mr. Mosley."

Marsters, listen to him?

"I'll tell you what, Mr. Mosley—if they don't say anything about the perishing wool, I will. I'll tell the beak. I'll say it's got to be looked into."

"You do that, Horace."

Mosley crossed the road away from him. This was not good. Mosley could see a situation festering at HQ. Tom Grimshaw, never a guaranteed ally, was going to be no use to him at all.

"Mr. Mosley!"

That was Millicent Millicheap, calling to him as if he were a friend whom she had given up hope of ever seeing again. She had been standing on a pavement edge, pondering about the cosmic purpose that had caused a yellow dry-cleaner's van to pull out and overtake a cyclist at a precise moment in eternity—a moment when A was standing here, B talking to C, and D looking into a shop-window. Could a bicycle fall in love with a yellow van? Could a yellow van feel contempt for a bicycle because it had tread-worn tyres?

"Oh, Mr. Mosley—I wish you'd been here the week before last."

"I'm sorry," Mosley said. "Things seem to have got a little out of hand."

"Oh, don't think I'm complaining. It was fun in a lot of ways—such an informative peep behind the scenes. Your Mr. Grimshaw is such a nice man—and Special Branch thrown in for good measure!"

"Special Branch?"

My God, who'd brought them into it? They wouldn't have cared much for that in Bradburn station.

"Yes—a very clever and charming man by the name of Wickham-Skeith. He has an almost psychic empathy with Gerard Manley Hopkins. And by the way, Mr. Mosley, the man from the Site hasn't been again. I'm rather glad, really. It would have been a bit much, if they'd taken me in for questioning again."

"I'll be getting these things straightened out, Miss Millicheap."

How? When? Where to start?

"And the man who was going to utter menaces—won't he be coming, either?"

"Not now, Miss Millicheap."

"Oh—I had been looking rather forward to him."

And then a practical angle of the situation struck her.

"You mean you're calling the whole thing off?"

"We'll be soft-pedalling—at least for the time being. For one reason or another, the moment is not propitious for an immediate follow-up."

"Well, you know best, Mr. Mosley. But I'm disappointed. And wasn't this all in aid of finding out what happened to poor Mr. Tunnicliffe? Have you abandoned that, too? Or perhaps you have found out in some different way?"

The flight across France and Spain. The bunch of flowers from the detergent company in their hotel bedroom on arrival. A sultry evening in Seville. The unique reality of standing in the courts of the Alhambra. *Rioja*. Warmth. Sunshine. Surf. A lot had happened to Mosley since he had first applied his working mind to Reuben Tunnicliffe.

"I really can't say yet," he said.

"I'll always be willing to help in any way I can."

"I know you will, Miss Millicheap."

So what now? The vicarage? Hang about their places of work in the hope of getting a word with one or other of the Rugger Buggers? In order, of course, to call off their activities? Mosley wondered how enthusiastically the Buggers had launched into their share of the action.

"Mr. Mosley!"

Someone else hailed him across the street as if he had returned after being reported missing on a polar expedition. Mosley did not want to talk to anyone else—but this was Deirdre Harrison. She crossed the road in front of an angrily braking lorry, looking herself rather like something obsolescent and home-serviced that had been on the road a long time.

"You went away at a bad moment, Mr. Mosely. You've missed all the fun."

Missed it? The fun wasn't going to start until he showed his nose back in the office.

"I think we've got it all worked out, though. Quite a scheme you had on. The only complication we haven't been able to work out is the vicarage. Was that or was it not part of your strategy?"

"I'm not quite sure what you mean," Mosley said.

"All right, then—be that way if you want to."

She said it without any trace of bitterness. A joke. The sort of joke they had made when they had worked with Mosley before. Mosley did not laugh.

"But I must say, once the Weskitts got started, they certainly went the distance."

"I'm not fully informed myself yet," Mosley admitted.

"Well, there's plenty to inform yourself about—though whether it will be the making or the undoing of your ecclesiastical friends, remains to be seen."

He knew that she would be able to fill him in about a lot, that her information would be wide-ranging and her judgement of it keen. But there was nowhere in Upper Crudshaw where they could hope to talk discreetly. She asked him what his immediate plans were, and he said that he intended to hang about and wait for the next bus back to Bradburn. At once she said she would run him there, and he accepted with a greater show of pleasure than anything else he had said to her this morning.

On the way she prattled uninterrupted about Willy Barber, Chief Inspector Marsters, Horace Kettle, Millicent Millicheap, Teddy Bemrose—and the vicarage. Two or three times she looked at him sideways, not convinced that he was listening. Was he going to stonewall every effort to get through his defences? When Mosley was stonewalling, it was like bowling to a last man in who was leaning on a bat four feet wide. Mosley's mood, in fact, was something that she had not experienced in him before—an introspection of which she would not have considered him capable.

The truth was that Mosley was disturbed—and it was the inner distress of a man who saw little hope of a way out. Among other things he was reflecting—as he had reflected often enough before—that it did not pay to go on leave.

He generally took his leave-allowance on a little-and-often basis, which saved him from having his current strategems uncovered by clots who could not be expected to leave well alone. But a leave as long as a fortnight had left his citadel undefended, and it was in a defenceless state that he was returning to HQ. He would be lucky not to be seriously disciplined, perhaps even shunted into some pre-retirement back-alley where they could consider him out of harm's way. And there was nothing he was going to be able to say to justify himself. There was no use pleading that things might have been different if he had been on hand to see them through.

He came to the conclusion that he must take the initiative and conduct his masters through his intentions from Square One—talk to Tom Grimshaw, perhaps with the ACC sitting in, if they wanted it as formal as that. That way, there would be no pretences for him to sustain. They would think he had gone off his rocker: but he had survived that misconception more than once in the past. This was different. He was not too certain himself that he had not gone over the top this time.

But at least he would tell them the plain truth. Then the slate—if they let him continue to own a slate—could perhaps be considered clean, if smeared.

Mosley was not given to worrying about the establishment; at least, he made a point never to appear to be worried. But if they were straining at the leash to move in on him—if, for instance, Marsters was helping to shape the whispers—he was in trouble that he could not afford to ignore. If they started to bully him—Mosley did his best not to speculate on how he might react to that.

"Do you think they're going to be very cross with you?" Deirdre asked suddenly.

"I beg your pardon?"

It was several sentences since he had heard anything she had said.

"Do you think they are going to be cross with you?"

"I'm fairly used to that."

That was the first lightish touch she had heard from him since they had met in the street. Only he did not make it sound very light.

* * *

As Deirdre Harrison was driving Mosley in through the
outskirts of Bradburn, a meeting was forgathering in the
big room over Wetherall's café in Upper Crudshaw—the
one that was used for wedding breakfasts and funeral teas.
It was not a big meeting, and the dozen women—all but
two of them aged more than fifty—looked somewhat insignificant against the emptiness of the background: the tres-
tle-tables had a primitive and unsafe air about them when
denuded of cloths. But there was nothing insignificant about
the voice of the formidable Miss Scratby as she rose to tell
them what they already knew: what they were here for.

"The first thing, ladies, is to elect someone to the chair."

And when Miss Scratby had safely cornered that honour
for herself, she outlined her thinking.

"Our first priority must be to collect evidence. I suggest
a rota to watch comings and goings, and to keep a careful
log of them."

Chapter Fourteen

Beamish continued to consider sheep.

One of the difficulties about the sheep was that there had been no apparent connection between the first few thefts. They had taken place in different neighbourhoods. They had been on a small scale. It took time for a common factor to emerge, and even then it was an uncertain common factor. The common factor was the manner in which the police had been decoyed, usually by an informer whose previous record had been unblemished—as such things go. Even Marsters, who was not given to making charitable allowances, had minuted that when Charlie Stableford had reported an overheard conversation about a projected raid on Barley Brow, he had genuinely believed that it was good stuff he was passing on. But then that might have been because Marsters would not readily admit that a grass of his could be a man of straw. What he had had to say to Charlie on the side was anybody's guess.

It looked on the surface as if the men on the recurring empty sheep-transporter must surely lead somewhere. But their tales of waiting about for the purchases that had not materialized had been checked, better checked and found frustratingly water-tight. They had been involved in impersonal agency contracts of the kind that did exist, and they had been paid their demurrage on the accepted scale. Local checks by out-of-town forces had confirmed all that the driver and his mate had claimed.

Beamish stewed over the file until he could have reproduced it from memory and came to a few working conclusions. Firstly, the raids were being mounted by someone clever who had a small and loyal team on call. Secondly, this someone was getting not only sheep but obvious amusement out of the battle he was waging with the law. And thirdly, it was someone local—someone who knew what the movements of sheep in the locality were going to be. There were a great number of sheep roaming unfenced moors, but it was not these untended flocks that were being depleted. It was when they were brought down for shearing, dipping or marketing that sheep were being spirited away. The rustlers could wait, it seemed, for the sheep to be brought to some gathering ground that suited them. And the director of operations was someone who knew what he needed to know about the working programmes of individual farmers. So Beamish thought he saw a possible approach. Who could pay false information to the villains that would lead them straight into an ambush manned by Beamish?

Mosley would be sure to have ideas about that.

Who was to know what was going on in the mind of the man in the shabby respectability of a black hat as he stumped along the narrow pavements behind the civic offices? Was he conceding the final victory of the humdrum after the timeless unreality of Mediterranean skies? Was he reflecting about the hypocritical solidity of Bradburn's nineteenth-century monuments after the white-walled mysteries of Moorish Spain? Mosley stepped crabwise to negotiate the wing of a vivid orange Mazda parked with two wheels over the kerb.

In the outer office conversations would stop short in mid-sentence when he came in. Even civilian callers who did not know him would be conscious that something special was about to happen. The eyes and ears of the most junior cadet would be tuned in on the imminent confrontation. How was Mosley going to react? Was this to be the battle that he had finally lost? Would he come back downstairs in half an hour's time, suspended, sent home to ponder the hints that he would be allowed to resign quietly, if only he would save the top floor the publicity of an in-depth investigation? And how would the legendary Mosley, the historic Mosley, Mosley the institution, respond to his disgrace? From the CID room windows his arrival would already have been noted. Men would be holding their fingers paused over their museumpiece Oliver typewriters.

But this was not quite how things turned out. Mosley came in through the outer office and was almost halfway across it before he was seen by anyone he knew. Only when he was almost at the inner door did Sergeant Hoskins at the desk look up and notice him.

"Mr. Mosley—"

He handed Mosley a letter, sealed in a typewritten buff envelope. Mosley carried it upstairs without looking at it.

"Nah, Jack."

"Nah, Fred."

Fred was a DI from S division whose existence Mosley had forgotten since before he had set out for Gatwick.

On his desk was a small stack of mail, mostly internal circulars and a rambling letter from an old girl in Carlow who sent him a bulletin of mostly imagined local criminalities every week. Last of all he opened the note that the desk-sergeant had handed him. Signed *Tom*, it was a brief and pally invitation to be in touch as soon as it suited him after his return.

"How was it, Mr. Mosley? We've all been hoping you'd have had one of those phoney posters done, advertising yourself as a bull-fighter. We've even cleared a bit of a wall to make room for it."

The breezy young DC who said that wondered why Mosley did no more than glower at him. Mosley hesitated to pick up the phone to ask for Grimshaw's secretary—but only momentarily. He had already made the operative decision. It was true that his confessional urge felt distinctly weaker than it had been two hours ago—but he was still determined that a clean breast should be his last thought on the matter.

Grimshaw received him with a broad smile, actually getting up and coming round his desk to extend a shakeable hand.

"You're looking fit, Jack."

"Aye. The sun shone. Wouldn't suit me out there in high summer."

Then followed awkwardness, both men temporarily unclued. Then both spoke together.

"There's—"

"If—"

And Mosley was quick to read the signs that this was not the prelude to a carpeting. True, there was a point up to which Grimshaw could be devious—or at least could try to be. Mosley put off for a minute or two the approach he had rehearsed.

"Has much been happening, Tom?"

"Not really. Business as usual on your patch. You know what that amounts to. I dare say you've been up there already, you bloody old rogue."

Very insistent, Special Branch had been, that nothing whatever was to be said or hinted that might alert Mosley to the fact that they had him in their sights.

"Cleared up the sheep business, have you?" Mosley asked.

"Not yet. Marsters is handling it. But he has chucked the work-load on to Beamish, so I'm hoping for a result soon."

"And you've nothing special for me?"

Grimshaw went through the act of giving special consideration to an unexpected question.

"I don't think so, Jack. Just carry on in your time-honoured way. Mooch about and pick up the threads. I'm sure you have the odd follow-up to do after two whole weeks."

Dismissed. Mosley went back to the detectives' room, looked up a few things in reference books, then went out by the back way, sidestepping between parked cars and merging with the neutral crowd in the centre of Bradburn.

"I gather he's back," the Assistant Chief Constable said.

"Yes. And there doesn't seem anything different about him," Grimshaw answered. "You wouldn't think he was a man with a time-fuse fizzing."

"He doesn't suspect we are on to him?"

"Apparently not."

"There are one or two little things," the ACC said, a phrase that his detective-superintendent always heard with dismay. Almost invariably they were the prelude to something that was going to ruin such of Grimshaw's day as was not ruined already.

"Wickham-Skeith has just returned the Horace Kettle file. He's had it ten days."

Grimshaw's hopes were raised. He could not think there could possibly be anything in the Kettle papers that would have made much impact on Wickham-Skeith.

"You'll remember that a fleece was found in the boiler-room. A fleece that Kettle claimed had been sent there for storage by Mosley."

"You want me to find out from Mosley—?"

"No! No, no, no, no, no! Under no circumstances. Mosley must not guess how much we know. Wickham-Skeith was adamant. But neither must we run the risk of the fleece being mentioned in court. Kettle is threatening to be bloody-minded about it, therefore Kettle must not come to court. The case must be withdrawn. Kettle must be let off with a caution."

"Less than a tragedy," Grimshaw ventured. "A carton of cigarettes is hardly the crime of the century."

"I'm glad you agree with me. Can I leave it to you, then, to let Marsters know?"

"I suppose so," Grimshaw said, hoping that he was suppressing all feeling from his voice. Marsters had put time, effort and vociferation into Horace Kettle. He was going to be memorably expressive about this waste of his time.

"I'm sure it will come better from you. You have a tactful way with men like Marsters. The second thing—" the ACC said.

Grimshaw hoped that he was not following his normal system of priorities and clearing minor matters out of the way first.

"The second thing, Tom, is sheep."

"Sheep."

"P division have had a go at them with Mosley attached. Marsters has had a go at them. Beamish is having a go at them at present."

"He'll clear it up," Grimshaw said brightly.

"I'm sure he will, Tom, but when? The Chief thinks—"

It always struck Grimshaw as remarkable how often the ACC ascribed his nastier thoughts to the Chief.

"The Chief thinks that you ought to take personal charge of this sheep thing yourself, Tom. He wants to be able to tell the press that our top man is commanding the operation in the field."

It was an order. There could be no counter-argument. For a self-revealing moment, Grimshaw was silenced.

"You can do it, Tom," the ACC said, in the tone of a scoutmaster encouraging a reluctant tenderfoot to work for a new badge.

Grimshaw set a firm chin and nodded.

"But it would be a pity to waste all the work Beamish has put in on it," he said. "I think I'll attach him to HQ for the duration of the exercise."

Wickham-Skeith was the first of various strangers to arrive in Upper Crudshaw. He had left behind him his umbrella, bowler-hat and morning suit and was now trying to render himself inconspicuous in a deer-stalker, a Norfolk jacket and riding-breeches of cavalry twill. He went straight to the Hanging Gate and claimed the room that had been booked for him by the travel specialists at his Branch office. Then he went and looked about the town, visiting among other shops the one that sold souvenirs to tourists. Here he bought a rugged staff of the sort that is known as a thumbstick, having quite obviously first toyed for several minutes with the notion of equipping himself for heavy outdoor activities with a shepherd's crook.

Chapter Fifteen

Millicent Millicheap knew she was liberated. She truly felt that she was on the verge of a verity. *Iguanas—Medicine Hat*—the man from the Site had taught her something, had shown her the new freedom to randomize that she had so narrowly and yet so absurdly missed all her life. She knew now that she herself, drawing only from her own resources, could do better than anything that the Early Warning traitor had produced from his world of skeletal masts and radar dishes.

> Hen-Len and Chicken-Licken sit in the back row
> Of dusty stalls
> With Poseidon and his blind-date partner.
> The dust from horses' hooves,
> Goodies and baddies alike,
> Obscures the Badlands—

"Cinema," the new poem was simply called, one of a new collection to be called *Key Words*, and to be published at her own expense if that was the only way to immortality.

"Cinema" was a poem about the pathos of escapism. She was weighing the rival random merits of *amphora* against *chrysoprase* when she heard the latch of her wrought iron gate and the faint flutter that was all that her front-door bell could produce from a fading battery.

It was a young man, perhaps in his thirties, wearing a Norfolk jacket and riding breeches and leaning slightly forward with his left thumb in the cleft of a rugged staff. She thought at first that this must be the man who had come to menace her. She felt a palpitation, then remembered that Mr. Mosley had said that this was not now going to happen. But then the man raised his deer-stalker, and she recognized Wickham-Skeith. Her heartbeat became more irregular still. She now felt as if she was on the brink of all the verities in the cosmos.

"May I come in, Miss Millicheap? There are one or two things I would love to follow up from our delicious conversation of the other day."

By the time she had made coffee he had read her poem, which was lying on her living-room table.

"Let me see if I can guess the key-words this time."

He had little difficulty with *Poseidon*, but wrongly suspected *Badlands*.

"Oh, no," she told him. "I am rather tempted to use *amphora* next."

"You are rather tempted? But hasn't the man from the Early Warning Site been more specific?"

"Oh, no. This is my own work. Mr. Mosley assures me that he won't be coming again."

Wickham-Skeith was careful not to wear the look of a man who thought he knew very well why that was.

"It is a pity, of course, because it means that now we may never know about Mr. Tunnicliffe."

"No?"

"You've heard of Mr. Tunnicliffe? He is the man who hanged himself from a nail in his outside lavatory. He always reminded me of an ant-eater. It is because of Mr. Tunnicliffe, you know, that all this has been happening."

"Yes. I have gathered that."

If Wickham-Skeith was now in an inextricable bog of mystification, he hid the fact by renewing his avid attention to Miss Millicheap's poem.

"You know, I envy you, Miss Millicheap."

"It is I who envy you, Mr. Wickham-Skeith. All those prizes in literary competitions. One day you are Ezra Pound, another Charles Causley, another Kathleen Raine—"

He shrugged his identities modestly off.

"Pure pastiche. Parody. Burlesque. I am chained to the rules set by the competition editor. Without them I could not compose a word. Whereas you—even without the man from the Site—"

He looked at her with a smile that turned her heart to sunwarmed butter. When he left he had in his possession a copy of "Cinema" in her own italic hand. It was going to give considerable trouble to MI8, the code-breakers. But they reached a firm interpretation of it in the end: an in-

terpretation that was to intensify activity in Upper Crudshaw.

Keeping secrets was both Teddy Bemrose's business and
his second nature. He always took it ill when he recognized
an attempt to prise a confidence from him and his character
was so well established in Upper Crudshaw that it was years
since anyone had tried.

When therefore an unintroduced young man came into
his office—a young man looking like a caricature of an Edwardian fell-walker, who said that he was an investigative
journalist trying to get to the bottom of recent events in
Crudshaw, the young man stood no chance at all. If, in fact,
Teddy Bemrose had had his wits truly about him, he might
have wondered what were the prospects in Fleet Street of
a reporter who could be got out of his office quite as easily
as Wickham-Skeith was. But the next person to call was
equally surprising: Reuben Tunnicliffe's daughter Susan who,
he had reason to know, patronized a Manchester lawyer.
She came to her point at once.

"I believe you are a friend of Inspector Mosley."

This was not the most propitious form of self-introduction
to Teddy Bemrose at the present time, especially as he was
convinced that she was a trouble-maker.

"I do know the officer," he said cautiously.

"Can you tell me how I can get in touch with him?"

Bemrose wondered whether he ought to pass on any
information at all to Susan Tunnicliffe. Asking Bemrose a
question was always tantamount to creating a new secret,
and he had become hyper-sensitive to anything that connected Mosley with Upper Crudshaw. Susan Tunnicliffe
looked at him keenly, sensing his hostility, and seeing no
immediate reason for it.

"You can contact him through any police station," Bemrose said.

"I dare say. But I could find him a good deal more quickly
if I knew which station he belonged to. Nobody at any
station I've phoned seems to know where he's likely to be."

Even at that Teddy Bemrose hesitated, as if every instinct
was warning him that the Tunnicliffe woman's sudden interest in Mosley was the fanfare for a finale of catastrophe.

She watched his Adam's apple rise and fall as if the exercise assisted his decision.

"He works from Bradburn," he told her at last.

"Thank you," she said with ironical courtesy, feeling as if she had expended a week's nervous energy to coax a professional confidentiality out of him.

Wickham-Skeith's first visit to Millicent Millicheap at Bradburn police station had alerted a chain of operatives, all hostile to each other, though none had so far risked an appearance in Upper Crudshaw. But they were clearly under their several starters' orders, and within two hours of Wickham-Skeith's visit to the town, they began to arrive.

A man with heavy eyebrows jutting out from under a fur hat booked in at the Hanging Gate. A casual man in a blue and white baseball cap sought and obtained a farmer's permission to pitch his light bivouac in a field on Crudshaw Nab. A ramrod-straight-backed man with staring eyes, finding the Gate now fully occupied, had no alternative but to accept one of the very basic letting-rooms at the Dog.

The vicarage at Upper Crudshaw had twelve bedrooms, no doubt its architect's tribute to the anticipated fertility of Wilfred Weskitt's nineteenth-century predecessors. It was a row of second-story windows, along the western elevation of the immense and robust stone-built mansion, that had provided the most prolific indications to Upper Crudshaw's moral standard-bearers that all was not meditation and prayer in the house of their incumbent.

There had been other spicily suggestive indications: the arrival severally or in pairs of half a dozen young ladies of a type one would not expect to see entering the incumbent's door, except perhaps in sack-clothed repentance of an abandoned existence. (It was two of these who had succeeded in silencing the habitués of the Dog while Beamish and Deirdre Harrison had been in the bar.)

What was more, once this cohort of over-painted, underdressed, and in one case nylon fun-furred young nubiles had disappeared within the hope-abandoning maw of the vicarage, they were never seen again in Upper Crudshaw. They did not re-emerge to explore what other amenities might be at their disposal in the vicinity. They did not come out to forage for convenience foods with which to supplement the vicarage's undoubtedly meanly stocked pantry. It was as if, once the vicarage had ingested them, they were being held to obscene ransom behind the upper windows of that western facade.

They were still there. Evidence of that was for all to see in the fluttering line of unvicarly garments that kept company with the Reverend Weskitt's next-Sunday surplice across the back lawn of the vicarage. Alongside it there danced lace-frilled bras, flimsy black princess slips, inadequate oriental pyjamas and one outfit of traditional schoolgirl uniform, including gym-slip and coarse black stockings.

Moreover, it was noticed that the vicar began to have frequent male callers, notably some of the more libertinous of the Rugger Buggers who, if they were coming for the resolution of their spiritual doubts, always seemed to put off doing so until after the landlords of the Dog and Hanging Gate had called time. At about half past eleven nightly they made their way, some of them furtively, along the vicarage drive. Then lights would go on, first behind the windows of the vicarage sitting-room, then behind the translucent violet curtains that had appeared in the western lattices. Music would descend from those windows—discord and cacophony to a lusty beat from some, and from others the sensuous close harmony of muted violins.

Florence Bray, spinster of the parish, was low in the pecking order of the recently recruited vigilantes, and therefore had to await patiently her turn for observation duty. Eventually, on a very dark and very chilly night, she found herself at her rostered post in the western shrubbery with notebook, torch and ball-point at the ready.

She hardly dared look towards those western windows. Florence Bray was a sheltered lady, and she quailed in advance before what her eyes might be going to see. Alice Hinchcliffe, on her evening's watch, had seen Mr. Richard Umbers arrive. She had seen him admitted by the front door, had heard women's voices, the vicar's wife's among them. She had seen the lights of the parlour go on, the curtains hastily drawn. She had heard a few bars of *Eine kleine Nachtmusik* played very loud on a radiogram, but this was quickly switched off and followed by what was known, she believed, as progressive rock.

At 11:50 (Alice Hinchcliffe had carefully noted the time) the music was turned off in the downstairs room, and lights now appeared in the windows of rooms four and five. (This numeration had been agreed on in committee under Miss Scratby's guidance.) Music now issued from behind those windows: massed choirs singing extravagantly scored Beatles' songs in room five and Hawaiian guitars in four.

What Miss Hinchcliffe saw thereafter had been reported to an extraordinary meeting of the society.

At 11:53 behind window five a woman pulled a blouse over her head, then had such difficulty getting her hands behind herself to the clip of her brassiere that a man came forward from within the room to do it for her. It was clear that he had no intention of limiting himself to being helpful. His hands wandered lasciviously and after an *obscenely close* embrace, the woman pushed him away and appeared to be pointing to his chest. He brought out a wallet from an inside pocket, and it was plain that money then changed hands.

The woman, however, appeared to be dissatisfied with what was being offered her, and after some gesticulation, the man produced his bank-roll a second time, after which the figures receded into the room and Alice Hinchcliffe was no longer able to make out their activities.

In the meanwhile, activity of a different kind was taking place behind window four. It was not specimens of *homo sapiens* but apparently two of the higher primates that were silhouetted against the curtains: protruding jaws and aggressively prominent eyebrows beneath shallowly descending foreheads—with long whippy tails erect behind the creatures' backs. Their first activity, however, was quite unlike anything observable in the animal kingdom. The two ape-like figures stood facing each other, each with their hands on the other's shoulders, and each looking into the other's eyes.

"I know," Miss Hinchcliffe told the committee, "that we are interested only in collecting evidence, and that we therefore must avoid at all costs arriving at unjustified conclusions, but I am practically certain that these were human beings got up as apes."

What happened next, however, only served to obscure this issue. For before she could avert her eyes, the couple seemed about to perform an act which, to her horror, she had once been compelled to watch on a *Wild Life* programme put out at a Sunday evening hour quite unsuitable for family viewing.

Florence Bray, shivering in the damp cold, saw nothing like any of this. No lights were on in the western windows. Such music as drifted faintly over to her from the house bore a distinct resemblance to oratorio. Shortly after eleven o'clock, there were signs that the Weskitts were going to bed. The music stopped. The front room lights were switched off. Light appeared behind an upstairs window, not one of those behind which previous watchers had been scandalized by what they had seen. There came the sounds of a late-night news bulletin being listened to on a bedside radio.

Then Florence Bray stiffened. Someone was coming along the crunchy gravel of the vicarage drive. She felt the adrenaline bristling in the small of her back. She could not see who the newcomer was, but his step was regular, firm, almost military. He came nowhere near her, went straight to the front door. She heard within the house the jangle of the manually operated bells. There was a short delay before lights appeared, first on a landing, then on the ground floor. The door opened, and Miss Bray saw in the light of the hall a tall, ramrod-backed man, addressing the vicar, who was in pyjamas and dressing-gown.

And at this moment, in another part of town, the landlord of the Dog was still laughing as he rinsed glasses and his wife swept the floor.

"It's the first time in my life a lodger has ever asked me outright to find him a woman. I sent him to the vicarage."

The Weskitts ate their breakfast under strain. Until now their agreements to differ had sometimes had to bridge gaps of daunting breadth and depth. But this time Cindy had gone too far and Wilfred felt himself driven back against that very wall from which she had hitherto always protected him: all the deadly considerations of status, dignity and the narrow rectitude expected of his calling.

It is said to be characteristic of clandestine situations that the one most closely involved is often the last to find out what has been happening in his own home. Wilfred Weskitt had been in blissful ignorance until last night. Then answering the door to a tall military man, who had asked him in forthright Teutonic gutturals to provide him *viz a voman*, had not been the ideal interruption to what he had had on with Cindy at that moment.

The Reverend Weskitt's Christianity became at once muscular and impulsive. He had ejected his caller from his threshold with a throw he had learned in a Judo club at his university. The man had picked himself up from the gravel and fled. Miss Bray had left the premises shortly afterwards.

Before going back to bed, Wilfred Weskitt did a little delayed thinking. There had been things going on in his house that had puzzled him, but that he had accepted at the face values offered to him. Not asking too many questions had been the easy way out: he blamed himself now for that. There were those young women that Cindy had claimed were old college friends down in their fortunes. They had stayed several nights, then apparently vanished in the small hours. There were those noisy visits by various of the Rugger Buggers who, Cindy claimed, were helping her in some forthcoming parish charity. And those visits had seemed to be centred on the embarrassingly vacant corridor in the western wing.

Wilfred Weskitt leaped up the vicarage staircase two treads at a time, flung open the doors of the offending bedrooms in quick succession. He had always believed these rooms to be empty and had conceived the plan of turning them into shelter for some category of the deprived. But he had made the mistake of passing his ideas along the proper channels. For more than two years now there had been obstruction and delay in one committee after another. There had even been a petition from an influential sector of Upper Crudshaw society that feared the influx of the deprived into their midst.

But now activities seemed to have been going on in those two rooms for which planning permission would certainly not have been granted. There was equipment lying about in two of them—screens made by stretching sheets between supports, two theatrical spotlights on stands and a selection

of cardboard cutouts suggesting a peep-show of unambiguous character.

Wilfred Weskitt was quick-thinking and by and large a
fair-minded man. He by no means understood all that was
happening, but he saw at once that the Rugger Buggers
could not be held primarily to blame. If the Rugger Buggers
had been here, operating this miscellany, then it was a case
of collusion. It was a case of more than collusion: it positively
smacked of Cindy's initiative.

Weskitt regularly forgave his wife for her divergence from
his opinions. As he had more than once told his congre-
gations he found her challenge astringent. He appreciated
her occasional pranks: they saved him from vegetating. She
rejected the values he believed in, yet respected him for
holding them.

But this was deception. This was underhand and sub-
versive.

It had already landed him with an anonymous letter that
was highly likely to be carboned to the archdeacon.

Last night, for the first time since their marriage, the
Weskitts had slept separately. Cindy, patient and farseeing
planner that she was, had seen that an immediate way out
was not going to be easy. She had never pushed Wilfred
as far as this before. She did not even feel that he was over-
reacting, but his entrenchment was deeper and firmer than
she had expected. And by now she had decided that this
breakfast table was not the ideal venue for a renegotiation
of their contract. At first she had hoped that a reconciliation
might happen accidentally, the way such things sometimes
do. But by the time they had disposed in silence of their
fruit juices, it was clear that it was not going to happen here
and now. It was with an unspoken acknowledgement of the
inexorability of fate that the Reverend Wilfred Weskitt tapped
his way into his four-minute egg.

Seconds later he was pushing it away from him.

"This one," he said, "is not even good in parts. It is
partially fledged. If this is your idea of a joke—"

She knew then that everything was stacked against her.

Chapter Sixteen

When Wickham-Skeith called on the Tunnicliffes, he found a household of varying activities. Annie Tunnicliffe, who had answered the door to him with a black smear across one temple, went straight back on her hands and knees in front of her kitchen range, to which she was applying black-lead with an urgency that suggested that her home had been singled out for royal visit later in the morning. In each of two fireside chairs a man was sitting. One of them was an elderly character, casual as to bedroom slippers and beige woollen cardigan (both once the property of Reuben Tunnicliffe) but immaculate even in his easygoingness. He was reading Gibbon's *Decline and Fall*. Wickham-Skeith took him to be Willy Barber.

At the other side of the hearth sat a man who had not yet shaved and who was making notes on the back page of his newspaper about the prospects of greyhounds. Wickham-Skeith had no idea who he was, being uninformed about an Irish connection. A museum-piece radio—one of the first sets designed to work direct from the mains—was reproducing a disc jockey's patter through a cackle of static. Against this background, at an all-purpose table in the middle of the room, Susan Tunnicliffe was writing in a music manuscript book, lost in reverie, excogitation or a desperate attempt to seal herself off from her environment.

"It's you he wants to see," Mrs. Tunnicliffe said.

The Irishman's lips moved silently as he spelled out to himself the name of a dog, and Willy Barber turned and smoothed a page as if he were unaware that anyone had come into the room. Susan Tunnicliffe unhurriedly finished a configuration of semi-quavers and made a note on a pad.

"Well, he's seen me now."

"I was hoping there'd be somewhere we could talk," Wickham-Skeith said.

"Well there isn't. There never has been in this house.

This room exists for domestic chores, family rows, imbecilic conversation and the composition of counter-point."

Wickham-Skeith, still looking as if he had been cast as Dr. Watson out on a rural case, came over to the table and looked knowledgeably over her work.

"A bold counter-subject, if I may say so."

"You may say so," she said, and closed the manuscript under his eyes.

"I wanted to talk to you about your father."

"By all means. There are two people present who did not know my father, but we have no personal secrets in this family."

Wickham-Skeith was still firmly gripping his thumb-stick rather like a child who fears that a toy is liable to be taken from him.

"What was the relationship between your father and Millicent Millicheap?"

Susan Tunnicliffe laughed—suddenly and spontaneously.

"I can't imagine. It would greatly surprise me if there ever was one. His tastes in women were catholic—but not infinite."

"Why has Inspector Mosley been taking such an interest in your father?"

"I would not venture to account for anything concerned with Inspector Mosley."

Wickham-Skeith paused, considered, apparently decided to carry on patiently.

"Would you have said that your father and Horace Kettle were friends, Miss Tunnicliffe?"

"I would have said that they barely knew each other, and that each of them considered that a satisfactory state of affairs."

"And Mr. Bemrose in the solicitor's office?"

"He is a clerk in a solicitor's office, and my father occasionally spoke to him about those things for which solicitors have clerks."

"Finally, Miss Tunnicliffe—was your father a churchman?"

"Chapel, actually. But he didn't go there either."

"So he never had a great deal to do with the vicar?"

"As far as I am aware, he had nothing whatever to do with the vicar. I cannot think what interests they could possibly have shared."

"What *did* interest your father, Miss Tunnicliffe?"

"As far as I have ever been able to discover, nothing."

"Did he know the vicar's wife?"

"He had noticed her."

"You seem to be in no doubt about that."

"He had spoken of her."

"Indeed? What did he say, Miss Tunnicliffe?"

"He said, 'Cor!' "

Wickham-Skeith had not risen to his eminence in Special Branch without learning fundamental facts about people. He realized that he was not going to get anything out of Susan Tunnicliffe in the present circumstances. He began to round off their conversation.

"I very much hope we shall meet again, Miss Tunnicliffe. I shall be most interested to see whether your second theme will next reappear in E flat major. A trifle audacious, perhaps, but that is where I would go."

"Far too remote a key," she said.

Beamish managed to make a viable if fleeting contact with Mosley, who was hurrying out of the office on some errand which he clearly did not want to talk about. Beamish asked him to recommend a contact who could be depended on to spread rumours about fictitious sheep movements.

"Nelson Brindley," Mosley said, without looking round to see who was talking to him.

"Ah—Mr. Mosley—"

Mosley did then turn, holding the main door half open, with himself half through it.

"I've never met this Brindley character. He's had sheep stolen himself, of course—"

"Good. That gives him a stake in it."

Mosley exited into the outer world—then spun absurdly on one heel and came back into the building.

"I will meet you at Nelson Brindley's, Sergeant Beamish. Shall we say the middle of this afternoon? But you must let me do the talking. Nelson is a suspicious man and he assumes all other men are as suspicious as he is. He expects to be suspected. He puts a lot of effort into hiding things he needn't hide. Get on the wrong side of Nelson, and you'll learn nothing from him for the rest of his life."

The dichotomy in Susan Tunnicliffe's soul went deeper than a simultaneous involvement with filigree baroque fugue and an Irish site foreman. Her difficulties had started when she had been born into a family like the Tunnicliffes and brought up in a home like theirs, imbued with their codes and standards, yet wrestling with a talent that was beyond the understanding of her parents, her brothers or any of their friends. The split had continued as she fought for her right to develop that talent. Even she herself had not truly grasped what the process was going to mean. There was no sympathy locally for the true nature of the problem. Her *cap and gown for music* were ultimately something that Upper Crudshaw was proud of—as if the right had somehow been conferred on the whole town to wear them. But initially her college career had been gossiped about in corners as a jumped-up notion.

Throughout her time at college she had been unable to organize her identity, all but totally incapable of reconciling her background with a society at which she secretly wanted to sneer. Her unique giftedness won the day, but when it came to making a post-graduate career at the college, there were cabals and intrigues against her by fastidious academics and aesthetes who did not think they could work alongside her. Add to this the robust sexuality that she had inherited from both sides of her parentage, her need for men and her innate contempt for them and Susan Tunnicliffe was not an easy woman for even herself to get on with.

Her first reaction to everything she encountered was contempt—contempt for anything appertaining to privilege and the self-convinced ruling class—which included the police. She had had nothing but scorn for Mosley when he had first called after her father's death. But for all her weaknesses, Susan Tunnicliffe quite often proved herself, in the final count, to be no fool. Sometimes she even seemed wise enough to know those weaknesses. She knew that her first impressions were frequently impulsive and unjust. And the more she thought about Mosley, the more was she fascinated by him. She could see that here was no ordinary policeman. She felt drawn to him as the rabbit is hypnotized by the stoat. So on the afternoon of the day on which Wickham-Skeith talked to her, she went to Bradburn.

Her first view of Bradburn police station did nothing to amend her opinion of the force in general. No one in Bradburn station knew where Mosley was. They asked each other where he might be, but she could see that that was a matter of form to show a stranger that they were at least trying. Some of them spoke as if they thought Mosley something of a comic cut. Others evidently regarded him with a certain gravity—but even that stopped short of respect. She demanded to see a senior officer, but came up at this point against all the combined skills of the outer office. If these men could have succeeded in protecting the general public as well as they protected their own upper echelons, there would have been no crime at all on the streets of Bradburn.

She was about to give up the cause as lost when a young plain-clothes man came down the stairs. He was fresh-faced, he was eager-eyed, he was bounding with an energy that told even in the way he bounded across the office.

"I don't suppose you know where Mosley is, Sergeant Beamish?" somebody asked him, maintaining the general pretence that losing a detective-inspector was not an everyday event.

Laughter.

Beamish simply shook his head and left the office with energetic strides. Susan Tunnicliffe followed him. It was a major athletic effort to catch him up. She managed it a hundred and fifty yards from the police station entrance. He looked down at her from his six feet with an expression of mixed impatience and distrust.

"Sergeant Beamish—I need to see Inspector Mosley."

He carefully weighed her up.

"It isn't something that I could help you with?"

"I'd rather talk direct to Mr. Mosley. He knows the basic facts."

"Not working today, Miss Tunnicliffe?"

"I do no teaching on Tuesdays and Thursdays. My mind

ought to be seething with counter-expositions and tonal answers, but it isn't. I've too much else on it."

They were standing now on one of Bradburn's narrowest pavements, had to move into a shop doorway to avoid pushing people into the traffic stream.

"Can you tell me anything about Willy Barber?" she asked suddenly.

He had to move again to let someone out of the shop.

"Only that a recent case against him had to be withdrawn."

"Even the local paper got to know that," she said sourly.

"It would be unprofessional of me to say more."

But she had the idea that Mosley would be bound by no such considerations. Mosley would have drawn up a professional code of his own years ago. She was aware of Beamish as a clean, and presumably clean-living, man at her side, a few years younger than her. Married? He was not wearing a ring—but then active young men like him often didn't. Not that she cared whether he was married or not. In her relationships with males she had always deliberately gone for those with whom there would be no involvement, emotional or economic, nothing that might threaten permanence.

"My mother and Willy Barber," she said, "are going to be married. That's what I wanted to talk to Mr. Mosley about."

"Yes, well, that's not a subject on which I would care to match my opinion against Inspector Mosley's."

Sergeant Beamish moved off. Susan Tunnicliffe came out of the shop doorway, and someone else bumped into her. It was Wickham-Skeith.

"Ah! Miss Tunnicliffe. A pot of tea in some mock Tudor decor, perhaps?"

"I wouldn't mind. I tried your modulation into E flat, by the way. It was most effective."

"Nostalgic?"

"Dreamlike."

Wickham-Skeith came out of the Assistant Chief Constable's room looking grave and pallid. He crossed the outer offices carrying his thumb-stick at the short trail and taking care to see no one. The ACC called at once for his detective-superintendent.

"Trouble, Tom."

"I knew there would be."

"I have just had a panful inverted over my head from a high altitude. It seems that Wickham-Skeith has seen Sergeant Beamish talking to Susan Tunnicliffe in a shop doorway. What is Beamish supposed to be doing with Susan Tunnicliffe? He's supposed to be helping you with sheep."

"I don't know. Perhaps he thinks he's traced some connection between Miss Tunnicliffe and the sheep-stealers."

The ACC seemed to regard this as beneath his consideration.

"We're supposed to be leaving everything severely alone that Special Branch have a finger in."

"I thought it was *laisser faire* as far as Mosley is concerned."

"Mosley, Tom—but not the rest of us. Wickham-Skeith wants me to discipline Beamish. How can anybody discipline Beamish? And in any case, it has just been made clear to me that Mosley is living in a fool's paradise—as are we all. Mosley had better make the most of his present flush of freedom. Did I not realize that at the end of the day Mosley is likely to go down for life—after a hearing in closed court? Wickham-Skeith seems to be under the impression now that the Irish are somehow involved. The possibility of a plot by the IRA cannot be discounted—or perhaps it is the loyalists. Also the Branch have men in Spain at this moment, going over every contact Mosley made there. The Costa del Crime, they call it; and where there is crime, Wickham-Skeith says, there are worse things going on. Even the *bona fides* of Mrs. Mosley's *All white, Jack* prize is being investigated."

The ACC unintentionally broke a plastic ruler.

"Tom, do you think we ought to have a private word and put Mosley on his guard?"

"I wonder if Mosley needs any warning?" Grimshaw said. "We can hardly sail in the teeth of orders, can we?"

The Assistant Chief Constable pouted.

"You know what I've always thought of Mosley, Tom."

"Indeed I do. And I've always thought you were a trifle—"

"This is hardly the time to go into that. My opinions haven't changed. But when all's said and done, he is one of ours."

Tom Grimshaw thought hard. The ACC became silent; perhaps he was thinking too. Finally, Grimshaw came to a conclusion.

"We can hardly warn Mosley direct. But I'll tell you what I'll do. I'll have an indiscreet word with Beamish about it. That will find its way home."

Chapter Seventeen

"Oh, Beamish—if I might have a word—"

Detective-Superintendent Grimshaw called Beamish back just as the sergeant was about to leave for his rendezvous with Mosley. But then, having got him into his room, he did not seem able to find anything to say. He made a closed circuit of a dozen bulldog clips, then unfastened them again.

"Things going well, these days, Beamish?"

"Yes. Just one or two frayed ends I wish we could tie up a little more smartly, sir. Sheep, for example."

"We shall get them, Beamish. We shall get them."

"Yes, sir."

"Seen much of Mosley since he came back from the sun, Beamish?"

"I've come across him briefly, sir."

"I wouldn't care to be in Mosley's shoes, Beamish."

"No, sir?"

"They're gunning for him, you know. Gunning for him. I find it very sad. He needs to be warned."

"Really, sir?"

"Special Branch, you know. They call nobody master. Law unto themselves. Respect no man."

"I suppose they have their job to do, sir."

"Yes, but—somebody needs to talk firmly to Mosley. Somebody he'll listen to: the sort of man who's worked on cases with him. Not many men have ever truly got to know Mosley, Beamish."

"No, sir."

"Whatever he's been up to, Mosley has got to drop it. He's got to detach himself. He's got to cover his tracks. Otherwise he's for it. Do you know he could even go down for a stretch, if they can prove the sort of indiscretion they suspect? The Chief and the ACC and I would be powerless."

"Sir."

"You'll be seeing Mosley before long, Beamish, I hope."

"I'm on my way to see him now, sir."

Tom Grimshaw wondered whether he had said too much or too little.

A helicopter flew in low over the Early Warning Station and then made a dozen circuits over Upper Crudshaw, during which tour it was deemed by the wise men of the town to have hovered specifically over Millicent Millicheap's, Annie Tunnicliffe's and the offices of Messrs. Aitken, Henderson and Brigg.

Within a week, a door-to-door salesman had offered almost every inhabitant an expensive aerial photograph of his delectable property, but Upper Crudshaw was not to be fooled by as bloodless a cover story as that. They knew in Crudshaw that an eye was being kept on the suspect traitors in their midst.

And in the meanwhile untrustworthy visitors continued to pour over the municipal boundaries. A rotund coachload of the Dutch sister organization of the Women's Institute created havoc by driving the wrong way along the one-way High Street in the face of Dicky Edmunds's milk-float, and its buxom matrons were suspected of every sedition in the calendar. Two Arabs in burnous and sandals failed to secure accommodation at the Dog, and a horde of motor-borne men in anoraks ambushed the vicarage with telephoto lenses.

And now the three international agents who had been the first to arrive at last got together. The gentleman in the enormous, peaked, blue and white baseball cap was Igor Stepanovich Chetverikov, who had on no less than three occasions successfully evaded recall in the later Stalin years. The man with the fur hat and the beetling eyebrows was Hiram C. Kincaid III, sometime Deputy Director of The Company's Sub-Arctic Division. And the ramrod-straight personage with the Teutonic accent and disposition, who had openly stated his intimate requirements at the vicarage door, was currently known as Pepe Pacifico. He was something of an adventurer and had to date served the interests of eleven of the shorter-lived Latin American republics.

The warp and weft of the trio's relationships had been the same in every theatre in which they had striven to outwit each other. For the first two or three days they invariably stalked each other round back-streets, public parks

and urinals. Then, inevitably, short of meat for the reports
that their masters were demanding of them, they came
together to bid and barter for such information as had come
the way of any of them. This was done with almost formal
ceremonial over a prolonged hand of Lofoten Skat, a card-
game of recondite complexity, which they had played in
their time in cafés on the Reeperbahn, along the Belsokorut
of Pest, the Prikopy of Prague—and more recently in the
shadow of the tomb of Sultan Baber of Kabul.

Upper Crudshaw, however, yielded no coffee-house suf-
ficiently atmospheric to do proper justice to Lofoten Skat.
So the three latter-day romantics decided on a country walk
instead.

Beamish had never ceased to be impressed by those acts
of defiance by which the yeomen farmers of Mosley's country had established their contempt for anything that life or
climate could ever try to do to them. They had sited their
strongholds as if with an eye to the maximum hardships of
inaccessibility and exposure. It was as if, knowing that the
combined ill-wills of topography and the elements were
steeply piled against them, they had surveyed the terrain
for the worst building plots that they could find. Perhaps
that gave them the consolation of knowing that any even
slightly descernible let-up in the animosity of environment
or weather would be something to rejoice about.

If that were the case, then Nelson Brindley's initiating
ancestor must have been the envy of his neighbours. It was
difficult to conceive of a more barren-looking acreage, of
stony fields more precipitously unworkable, of a dwelling
less sheltered or more remote from any other—or more
difficult to reach from any macadamed road.

But there were some advantages that a man minded as
Brindley was said to be could derive from the stark insu-
perability of his situation: he had long notice of any stranger's approach. He occupied the top of a hill, backed by a
discontinued quarry-face, so that access from the rear was
reserved to rock-climbers undaunted by the vertical. On
his front and flanks he commanded a view that fell away for
at least a mile in every direction, a landscape without hedges,
with low walls broken by many a gap and almost entirely

denuded of trees. It thus afforded no cover even to a man crawling upwards on his stomach. Nelson Brindley's security was as reliable as that of any medieval brigand on his castled crag in the Rhine gorge.

But, Beamish reflected, as his rear suspension jibbed at the demands made on it by Brindley's neglected dirt-road, it was highly unlikely that the farmer would be watching his front at this moment. Mosley was already with him, and would be keeping him occupied. Beamish could see the unmistakable lines of Mosley's Ford Popular parked against the wall of Brindley's farmyard. (It was axiomatic that Mosley would never use his own car on duty except in cases of last-ditch urgency.)

But Brindley was out looking nevertheless, leaning over his gate, his one eye working over Beamish with a feverish restlessness. (He wore no patch or artificial pupil to hide the disfigurement of his vacant left socket, a wrinkled concavity at the centre of which there appeared to be a small hole.)

"Is Mr. Mosley about?" Beamish asked.

"He was a minute ago," Nelson Brindley said, as if that were no guarantee of anything. Beamish was quickly to learn that straight answers to simple questions were not Brindley's way of life: his dedicated purpose at all times was to mislead all men about all things. But this did not necessarily mean that he had anything to hide. Hiding things had been his habit for years.

"I'd like a word with him, now I've come. Do you mind if I come into your yard?"

"I'm not stopping you," Brindley said.

"Where is Mr. Mosley, then? Is he in the house?"

"Not to my knowledge."

Beamish went to peep over the half-door of a sty.

"I'd be glad if you didn't go about disturbing things. That animal's sick."

He seemed as anxious to keep Beamish away from the sty as if he had an illicit still in there. Beamish saw the dangers of offending him.

The yard was in barely describable disorder, littered with agricultural machinery for which Beamish knew neither the names nor the purpose. It was hard to know whether gen-

erations of Brindleys had been loth ever to let anything go
to the scrap-yard or whether this mud-logged and rusting
heap of spikes, wheels, cogs, bolts, chains and rollers was
the present husbandman's working equipment.

There was also a breath-stopping smell about the place
ad it quickly became apparent that Brindley himself was
one of the principal sources of it. Beamish looked round for
a diplomatic excuse to sidestep to windward of him.

He then saw that Brindley's work for the afternoon, in
which he had presumably been interrupted by Mosley's
arrival, had been hosing down the interior of a motor-tanker
of the kind that is used for emptying cesspits and slurry
from cowsheds and the like. Mosley later told Beamish that
one of Brindley's diversifications, in view of the parlous
productivity of his holding, was performing this service for
neighbours who were as remote as himself from sewage
systems.

Beamish was not tempted to go anywhere near this vehicle, but wondered what excuse Brindley would find to
keep him away from it if he appeared to be showing an
interest.

"I believe that you've had some sheep stolen, Mr. Brindley?"

"That's been dealt with," Brindley said. "In every re-
spect, that is, except getting me my sheep back. Your man
Marsters was here. He asked me every question in the book.
I'm not answering any more."

"That's not what I'm here for. I'm here to talk to Mr.
Mosley. Where is he?"

Brindley was clearly worried by the same question. He
looked uneasily behind himself. But Mosley chose that moment to reappear, coming round the corner from a line of
outhouses wearing the blank expression of a man who does
not know that he has done anything likely to create alarm
and irascibility. Beamish could see what must have happened. Mosley would have been holding the farmer in a
keen and disturbed conversation—everything disturbed
Brindley—when they heard Beamish's bottom gear struggling with surface and gradient. Brindley would have broken off the talk to go and look—he always went to look.

Mosley had seized the opportunity to do a little harmless snooping.

Brindley swivelled his eye on to Mosley. He had only the one optic, but it could be as expressive as any average four of its kind. It took aim at Mosley with a prime distillate of irascibility. But he held his tongue. Brindley knew only too well Mosley's rank and potential.

"Funny thing I saw just now, as I was coming back from a pee, Nelson."

"What was that, then?"

"I just happened to look into a shed, and what did I see but three men drinking a pot of tea and playing cards on a bale of straw."

Brindley had no answer ready, and Mosley gave him no time to think of one.

"Oh, don't worry, Nelson. I know you make tea for walkers and that. But why are you so dead scared about it? Do you thing I'm going to report you to the Revenue for undeclared income, or something?"

Brindley muttered something about not being able to trust anybody these days.

And who would accept refreshment at the hands of Nelson Brindley, fresh from his muck-cart? One had to assume that there was a woman about the establishment somewhere: a sobering thought.

"This is Sergeant Beamish, who's also after the sheep-thieves. Like me, he wants to know all he can about local flock-movements in the near future."

So Mosley had already started planting ideas into Brindley's head—but he had gone a stage further than Beamish's plan. He was after real sheep movements, as well as fictitious ones. And—he assured Beamish when they met again, down on the main road—Brindley was a gossip. After his fourth or fifth pint during the extended licensing hours of market day, he was a man who could talk: just as long as it was not his own affairs he was talking about, and just as long as he was spreading nerves and anxiety of some kind or other.

Beamish and Mosley sat in Beamish's car, having rounded a bend that concealed them at last from Brindley's line of vision.

"They're worried about you, back at HQ," Beamish said.

"Oh, aye? They've been worried about me since I joined."

"I think they feel," Beamish said, "that this has got outside their control—that you're going to be used as a scapegoat."

"I suppose, in a mild sort of way, I could be said to have broken the law."

"In a *mild* sort of way?"

"I did inspire a few little rumours, to see who would react to them."

"*Little* rumours?"

Mosley fell unusually silent. Beamish drove on for some miles without interrupting whatever line of thought he was following.

"I believe," Mosley said unexpectedly, looking out of the window at sheep on a high ridge, "that those are Border Leicesters that Joe Pegler is running with his Wensleydales."

Beamish came as near to being exasperated as he had been the first day he had met Mosley.

"Inspector Mosley—Mr. Mosley—*Jack*: I don't think you fully realize what trouble they might try to make for you. These men from the Branch—and all the various straphangers who keep appearing all over the place: they have powers such as you and I have never imagined."

"I can see that they may need thoughtful handling," Mosley said. "We shall have to see if we can mix them a bottle."

That was the moment at which Beamish decided there was no more he could do.

Romance at various stages was in the air in Bradburn as well as Upper Crudshaw.

Susan Tunnicliffe was drinking tea and eating buttered toast with Wickham-Skeith in the Tudor Café, well aware that this was suddenly one of the critical moments of her life, if not destined to be the turning-point of everything. It was as if time itself had called for a *rubato*, a new tempo, a new rhythmn, bringing her an acute new awareness of the shapes and shades of teacups and ashtrays, of the view across the roof-tops and the short hairs at the nape of a waitress's neck.

It was true that Wickham-Skeith looked a bit of an ass in his notionary countryman's garb. But she had to admit that when she had caught sight of herself in a shop-window mirror half an hour ago, she had been very angry with herself at the few clothes she had brought with her from Manchester.

Wickham-Skeith hummed his E-flat counter-suggestion to her over the table. It was not only his musical knowledge that had taken her by surprise. The man was civilized. Things that were hard-fought-for specialisms in other people were mere sidelines to Wickham-Skeith. He even let fall the hint that on free Saturday afternoons he could still pull his weight behind an oar in a light four on the Upper Thames. Susan Tunnicliffe wondered what he could do with his weight on a waterbed.

Also under the spell of Wickham-Skeith was Millicent Millicheap, who had started experimenting with a new kind of poetry. It had passable sentences and metaphors that began and ended where you could see them. Her current (unfinished) effort was about Pennine winds and honest tweeds.

The sonnet was unfinished because she had decided on impulse to go out and buy herself a home perm. But she had begun to use it having read only half the instructions on the packet. She must have gone wrong somewhere, she decided, for she was in danger of asphyxiation by the most nauseating smell that had ever assaulted her. She thought she would never be able to get it out of her clothes.

That evening Beamish and Deirdre Harrison sat under the inside wall of Hadley Dale churchyard eating chips they had bought from a mobile fish-frier in the village square. A subtle change had come over their relationship, though they were too close to it to recognize it themselves. Deirdre did not swear very much these days, but latterly, if she had felt like swearing in Beamish's presence, she had sworn. And Beamish was no longer taking care not to talk pompously in Deirdre's presence. If a touch of pomp suited the point he was making—which was not often nowadays—he was not afraid to produce it. In other words, they had both started being natural in each other's company.

They were, of course, discussing Mosley.

"At the lowest level, they might try to do him for creating a public mischief—wasting police time," Beamish said.

"He hasn't wasted police time. Other people have done that."

"Yes—but I know Mosley. There are people he'll be loyal to."

"Let's hope you're one of them. I don't want you getting too deeply involved in this," Deirdre said. "You've too much to lose. Mosley knows that and he'd be the last one to want you to."

"*We've* too much to lose," Beamish said.

Annie Tunnicliffe and Willy Barber were eating smoky-bacon flavoured crisps in the Old English Gentleman at Cowburn. Barber's eyes wandered professionally over a neatly dressed and not too elderly widow eating alone in a corner, and evidently a resident.

"Eyes front!" Annie told him.

"I was just thinking. There was a time when—"

"Please yourself. But remember what I've told you. If you get yourself another dollop of time, I shall not come visiting you. I shall probably be glad of the rest, anyway."

Mike Maguire sat in the Dog at Upper Crudshaw with the clear intention of getting as drunk as he could as rapidly as he could. He had correctly read the glitter in Susan Tunnicliffe's eye when she had come back late that afternoon from her tea-sipping caper in Bradburn. And she had gone out again this evening putting on one of her highly resolute feminist acts; she would have spat like a cat if he had asked her where she was going.

Mike Maguire knew when there was writing-off to be done.

Chapter Eighteen

The Mosley home was not known to many outside their own small circle. It was not that the Mosleys were inhospitable. It was simply that the pressures of work left little time for entertaining colleagues.

It was a comfortable Edwardian property—Mrs. Mosley was reputed to have brought a little money to the marriage—and though there were neither fields nor woods between their avenue and the town, there was a feeling of pastoral retreat once one was within their green gate. The Mosleys had no more than a pocket handkerchief of lawn, seldom closely mown, but its small expanse seemed to seal off the world of Interim Crime Reports, the ACC and even Special Branch.

Cindy Weskitt came along the Avenue early in the evening, half an hour after Mosley had finished his supper. She was carrying a small suitcase that she had considered light when she had set out with it, for the Weskitts were not a two car family and she did not propose to go back to the vicarage after talking to Mosley. She had not thought she had time to go down to the railway station to park the suitcase there, though actually, she had the evening ahead of her: Mrs. Weskitt was, uncharacteristically, too disorganized to think properly.

The Mosleys both took note of the suitcase as she set it down in their hall; neither said anything about it. Cindy Weskitt was pale, and the smile that she evidently regarded as *de rigueur* was so artificial that it seemed to be fixed. There was nothing sexy about her at all.

Mrs. Mosley was a jolly woman when she appeared at the unavoidable annual rituals of the force, but she was the epitome of sympathy and concern within her own home; she could appear to know everything or nothing according to the exigencies of the context.

Mosley was in carpet slippers, which gave him an air of being off duty—Mosley, who many thought never allowed himself to be off duty. Cindy Weskitt was highly sensitive to this, and apologized with genuine regret for disturbing his leisure. She was not sure whether Mosley waved this aside as he showed her to a chair.

"I'm afraid I let everything run away with me," she said.

But if she expected Mosley to say something immediately consoling, she was immediately disappointed, for he had nothing to say at all.

"I just didn't foresee how things would turn out."

"Then you can't have looked at them very closely," Mosley said.

"I accept your rebuke,"

"Then while you are in the mood for rebuke, I will tell you one or two things that I have on my mind."

"Please do."

But Mosley was not going to allow his schoolmasterly gravity to be punctured by soft answers.

"Before I left home for two weeks, I persuaded three people to do unusual tasks for me. And I asked you to keep an unobtrusive eye on things, because I mistakenly thought I could trust your common sense."

How much more hurtful was he going to be before he had finished?

"I gave Millicent Millicheap a small handful of counterfeit coins to pass off on local tradesmen—a few to the milkman, one or two in the supermarket, a few in the paper shop. In doing this, I was compounding a crime: the law's always humourless when anyone monkeys about with the national currency. It's true that the value of the money concerned amounted in all to less than one pound sterling: but whether that would have been a mitigating circumstance is a moot point—especially when a serving policeman is involved. However, I suggest that in this instance the end definitely justified the means. I was trying to find out what drove an honest man to suicide. Miss Millicheap was going to transgress so often that word would get round—and people would start asking themselves whether this might not be accidental. My hope—I'll admit it was rather a thin one—was that a petty blackmailer would try his luck and give himself away. As I say, I doubt whether it would have worked. That was why I backed it up with other case-histories."

"I was sure it wouldn't work," Cindy Weskitt said, not undemurely. "That was why I brought in the business of the Early Warning Station."

"And who did the groundwork for that? Who was it that called on Miss Millicheap and gave her her famous key-words?"

"My brother. He's not known in Upper Crudshaw, and happened to be in Leeds for ten days or so of business talks."

"Is he likely to visit Upper Crudshaw again in the near future?"

"Most unlikely."

"You'd better make sure he doesn't."

"He is actually overseas at the moment."

"He'd do well to stay there, if he wants to avoid being arrested on sight. Oh, he'd probably be able to talk his way out of it—eventually. But by that time, he'd have had several months of aggravation—and any number of other people would have been caught up in the wearisome business. And it's far from certain that he'd get away with it, even then. There are people working on this case now who won't want to leave it without a result."

"But if all we're going to do is to concoct a cover-up—"

"That will be a lot better than the most probable alternative."

This was the first relatively cheerful thing he had said since she had come into his house, his first suggestion that he had not given up hope of a way out.

"I'll answer for my brother," she said.

"And so we come to a gentleman whom I used to count among my friends. Mr. Edward Bemrose. I'd thought of asking him to keep watch over events during my absence. But I thought that perhaps he might perhaps be just a little too heavy-moving—"

"That's what I thought. That's why I—"

"Let your sense of humour run amok," Mosley completed for her, in a tone of ruthless irrevocability. "Old Ted had agreed—not too happily, I'll admit—to let it be believed that he was using his masters' Upper Crudshaw office as a base for selling racing tips. I would ultimately have cleared it with the partners. They'd have had a good laugh about it. But when it comes to the sort of thing you started advertising on his behalf in the telephone box—"

"I'm sorry, Mr. Mosley, but I honestly thought it had a better chance of working. I'm still rather surprised that it didn't."

"In Upper Crudshaw? Heavy breathing? Coy little whimpers of delight? Why, when I was a young man—"

"Oh, Mr. Mosley, please don't read me that kind of lecture. I sincerely believe you're deluded about the way things were in your youth. That was what all this was basically about—at least as far as Wilfred and I were concerned."

"May we leave your family life out of it for the time being? I don't propose to express any opinions about the state of things between you and your husband. Let's come to Horace Kettle. That is at least one case that you didn't interfere with—and he only escaped the dock by a stroke of good fortune that hasn't done the rest of us any good."

"By your own admission, I had nothing to do with that."

"No. I take the full blame for it. I sent a fleece for him to mind, at a time when anything to do with sheep is a hot property in these parts."

"I don't understand you, Mr. Mosley. First you blame me, than you blame yourself. Whose side are you actually on?"

"Just for once, on my own side, struggling to find a way of squaring all this up. But after the way you went to town on your own doorstep—"

"I know. I must have gone mad."

"I asked you to let the tale trickle round that your vicarage was being used for some highly staked card play involving the Rugby Club. I didn't ask for shadowgraphs and slapstick pornography."

"I got carried away."

"I'm not given to moralizing as a rule, Mrs. Weskitt—but you have a dangerous sense of fun."

"You're quite right, of course. But may I say a little more about it than that—*please*? There was more to it than fun. At the time, it seemed a logical process."

"I never had the advantage of formal training in philosophy," Mosley said. "So what I know about logic is mostly self-taught."

"How can I explain? I think it's only now that I've realized that we're not college students any more—that the world we are in is not the one we were looking out at when we were nineteen or twenty."

"It never was," Mosley muttered.

"Wilfred and I don't really differ as much as the outside world thinks we do. We exaggerate—because exaggeration itself is a teaching method. That's what we are, fundamentally, teachers—trying to get people to look critically at their sense of values, trying to startle them into new judgements. Somebody—I think it was G.K. Chesterton—once said that the most effective way of teaching is from stupid examples. It's not unlike being devil's advocate. After all, the role of devil's advocate is essential to the process of making someone a saint. Do you see what I'm trying to say?"

"I think I know what you may mean. But that kind of word-game is all right among people of like mind. You can't expect the real world to understand it. In Upper Crudshaw they can't make head or tail of it. And in the cathedral close—"

"Don't twist the knife, Mr. Mosley. It's been round in the wound several thousand times in the last few days."

And she began to cry, so silently at first that an objective observer might have been mistaken about the intensity of her distress. Mosley was patient and unembarrassed. Presently he brought out a large, curved-stemmed pipe, from which he produced a great volume of blue smoke.

"Now Wilfred doesn't want to know me. He's said very little—nothing you could call positive. His silence is worse than any words he could put his tongue to. I know what he's thinking—and I can't stand another hour of it. I've come away. I don't know how I can handle any of this."

It was an invitation to Mosley to provide his solution—or at least to act as a baffle to her thinking. But he made no offer, said nothing to make her problems easier.

"I'm sorry if I'm wasting your time, Mr. Mosley—saturating your leisure with my misery."

For long moments it seemed as if he was not going to make any comment, even to that.

"I think you're a lucky woman," he said, after the pause.

"I don't know how you make that out."

"From the way you're behaving, I'd say it's the first time anything's ever gone wrong in your life."

She looked at him without immediate understanding.

"It will have done you no harm in the long run."

"But what can I *do*?"

"You could go home and talk to your husband as you've just been talking to me."

Cindy Weskitt sighed.

"How easy it is to lose sight of one's target. This all started over Reuben Tunnicliffe. We seem to have forgotten him in the process. We are no wiser about him, are we?"

"Aren't we?"

"You mean you are? You've discovered something?"

"Every day we're all a little wiser about something," Mosley said enigmatically.

"Or a little more foolish."

She sat back in her chair and closed her eyes, pale still, but calmer, as if talking to Mosley had drained her of some of the poisons of conflict.

"Mr. Mosley, I feel as if I've grown up in the last half hour. If only I thought there was some way of getting Wilfred to see that I've grown up—"

"You won't convince him of anything by sitting here talking to me," Mosley said.

"No. I'll go back home. May I ring for a taxi?"

Mosley got up from his chair, his limbs moving tiredly.

"I'll run you up to Crudshaw, Mrs. Weskitt."

Michael Maguire was a sentimental man. That was why he was also a fighting man. If it is true that alcohol undoes repressions and inhibitions in the reverse order from which they are acquired, the more recent ones first, then any control that Maguire had learned to operate over his aggressive instincts dated from not much earlier than yesterday. He had wanted to start a fight in the Dog, though his reason for taking offence was unclear to anyone but himself. But his pugnacity was no problem in the Dog. Someone he did not see put a half-Nelson on him, someone moved a chair out of the way, someone opened the street door and

Maguire reeled into the cool air of Upper Crudshaw, swearing repetitively and dazed.

He went to the Hanging Gate, where he would not have been served, had not an inexperienced young barmaid failed to recognize the condition he was in. Chetverikov, Kincaid III and Pepe Pacifico were also in the Gate and Maguire sensed at once that here were three men whose potential interest widely surpassed anything else he was likely to encounter in Crudshaw. He addressed them across the room, demanding their views on local government power-sharing in County Armagh. Their unreadiness to commit themselves appeared to offend him more than any partisan opinion might have done. Maguire began to remove his jacket.

Action followed fast. Management called in the law, and the law was close at hand, since two young constables in a patrol car were cruising near to Upper Crudshaw as a supplementary back-up force in whatever contingency plans Wickham-Skeith had up his sleeve.

They were under strict injunction to ignore anything that Chetverikov, Kincaid III or Pacifico might appear to be up to, but no one had said anything to them about Maguire. They told Maguire they were going to take him in—which cost considerable damage to their shins, rib-cages and uniforms.

As they were getting him into their Panda, Mosley came alongside in his Popular.

Chapter Nineteen

There was something radically amiss with Millicent Millicheap's house. A solid suffocating wave hit Wickham-Skeith
as she opened her front door to him. It was the most chok-
ing, the most emetic, the most intolerable smell that had
ever come his way in his undercover service to the state.
But Wickham-Skeith's sense of duty was strong. He had to
penetrate into this woman's home. He had to walk into this
wall of nausea and potential asphyxiation.

Then he saw that something was even more amiss with
Miss Millicheap herself. Something radical seemed to have
happened to her hair. Instead of lying in enticing soft curls
across her scalp, as she had intended, making her look as
if she had stepped from an early 1930ish advertisement for
suburban housing, it hung lank and sodden in a straight
curtain that started over her eyes and clung unevenly round
four fifths of the circumference. Perhaps she had used too
much of the stuff in the packet (somehow or other she had
used it all) or perhaps the stuff had deteriorated on the
chemist's shelf. Or perhaps this was one of those cases
where ingenious management criminals had substituted an
inferior compound for a branded product.

Miss Millicheap was herself undergoing physical changes
at the sight of Wickham-Skeith—a weakening of her knees,
the apparent substitution of water for blood in the arteries
of her legs and a prickling of adrenaline throughout her
upper regions. She was also aware that she was not in
the state in which she would have chosen to receive this
man. And Wickham-Skeith learned, as he approached
her, that the obnoxious fumes that supercharged her hall-
way appeared to be emanating from the woman herself:
from the ludicrous dank fringe that hung about her face
and neck, and from the patches of the revolting solution
that had soaked into her amorphous unbuttoned navy blue
cardigan.

But duty sometimes had to face worse perils than bullets.

"Do you mind if I come in, Miss Millicheap? This is important."

"Of course—Do you think I might go upstairs and put a towel round my head, Mr. Wickham-Skeith?"

"Please do."

Her living-room, no less than the rest of the house, was an acrid pocket of unbreathable air. Wickham-Skeith tried to open a window, succeeded only in catching the back of his hand across a fly-paper.

On the table, as always, lay a poem in mid-transcription. Wickham-Skeith moved over and read it. But it was not in Miss Millicheap's usual style. It lacked verve, it lacked imagination, in particular it lacked random tangents.

As I watch your straight-limbed stride across the moors,
My heart identifies with all that's yours.

Wickham-Skeith had no idea that he was reading about himself.

When Miss Millichcap came back downstairs, she was wearing an already sodden turban. Wickham-Skeith had decided that his only plan must be to get through with his business and make himself scarce. Nevertheless good breeding demanded that he should not come down to the nitty-gritty without some semblance of cultural prelude.

"Have you seen this week's issue of the *Times Literary Supplement*, Miss Millicheap?"

"I'm afraid it has not been delivered," she said. "That happens sometimes in these wilds."

It happened every week, as a matter of fact, since she had no standing order for it.

"There was a sequence of triolets about solid geometry that I thought might appeal to you. I'll save mine for you."

"Oh, you are so kind."

She smiled at him, but he appeared not to be looking directly at her.

"Miss Millicheap, I want you to put another poem in the newspaper for me this week."

"Oh, dear—oh, yes—of course—by all means—"

"I'm not asking for inroads into your valuable time. I've taken the liberty of writing a poem for you."

Because the code-breakers, devoted men who claimed never to have failed, men who could crack ciphers under shell-fire and spot duff groups in the teeth of mortal exposure, had succeeded in making sense of the iguanas and varnished hatpins, the random excursions to Zurich and Medicine Hat, and had proved to Wickham-Skeith's appalled satisfaction that the Eastern Bloc now knew enough technicalities about what was going on on Crudshaw Nab to jam the Early Warning System into immobility—or set its networks crackling with misleading warnings as preferred.

Wickham-Skeith laid his poem on the table.

Ankle-deep in guano,
I square my shoulders, scatter my leopard's spots
Like mistral-driven, frequency-modulated
Poplar down,
Across a *Plaza* named after one of Franco's generals.

"It's beautiful," she said. "But I can't put my name to something that isn't mine."

"There are sacrifices that we are all called on to make if our civilization is to survive."

The air of Upper Crudshaw was good as he let himself into the street. He drew deep gulps of it.

Mosley was coming away from the vicarage when he saw the patrol arresting Mike Maguire. He had carried Cindy Weskitt's suitcase up to the vicarage door and had rung the bell for her, since she had come away without a key, not thinking in her misery that she would ever be returning.

It was some time before there was any answer. Then there was a drawing of bolts and a fiddling with the latch, then a palefaced Wilfred Weskitt was standing in front of them in an antique but really rather chic quilted housecoat. He turned his back on them and walked away into the depths of the house, leaving the door wide open behind him. Mosley signalled to Cindy to follow him and himself turned away and got into his car.

In Upper Crudshaw High Street he pulled up ahead of the Panda and waited until he had seen the two constables safely install a manacled Maguire inside it. Then he walked back to them, his coat open, and the man in the driving-seat lowered his window.

"Get him to hospital at once. Don't book him till they declare him sober—which won't be tonight. I don't want to lose this man through alcoholic poisoning. I need him as a key witness. Make sure it's noted in the Incident Book that he is not to be let out on bail till I've had a word with him."

"Sir."

Neither officer had heard Mosley speak as incisively as this before, though it was recorded in the mythology of the force that he had been known to do so. He turned away from them and went into the Hanging Gate.

Kincaid III, Chetverikov and Pacifico were sitting together at a table that seemed to set them apart from the largely middle-class clientele of the pub. Middle-class conversation this evening had become subdued and in some groups had petered out altogether. They had not spoken to any of these men, but there was no doubt in the folk-mind as to what sort of men they were.

The men themselves were morose, which came partly from their abject failure to discover anything, even in concert, that they could report back to their opposing bases. It also derived from the large number of formal, sentimental and insincere toasts that they had drunk to each other's causes in neat gin.

But a slight ripple of new consciousness quickened their veins when they saw Mosley come in. The Russian passed round a packet of rice-paper cigarettes. The American signed with his eyes to the bar that they wanted another round. Pacifico slid down his fingers to make sure his flies were buttoned—a compulsive gesture that he made every few minutes. None of them had so far met Mosley to speak to. They firmly believed that he was the vital figure in this affair, but even a pooling of their theories had not produced a notion about what his part in events could possibly be.

Mosley bought himself an old-fashioned blend of mild and bitter and carried it over to their table.

"Mind if I join you, gentlemen?"

There was a concerted haste to make room for him. Mosley took off his hat. Chetverikov offered him a cigarette, which he accepted, and which the other two lit for him. There was something almost obscenely unnatural in the sight of Mosley behind a cigarette.

"I've a feeling that I've seen you three gentlemen before," Mosley said. "Were you not taking tea the other day at my friend Mr. Brindley's place?"

"Tea—?"

Then the American bethought himself that it might be diplomatic not to be too critical of a national institution. "Tea? Yes, I suppose it qualified to be called that. It was an infusion that had distant roots in a far eastern plantation somewhere."

"His wife makes tolerable cake," Pacifico said.

"I would say that they are a couple who are perfectly suited to each other," was Chetverikov's contribution.

"And what did you make of my old friend Brindley himself?"

"I would say he is a most English character."

"I have never known a man work so hard to clean out what you call a sheet-cart," Pacifico said.

"A man must have character to persevere on that hillside."

"There's no need to lean over backwards looking for nice things to say," Mosley told them. "When I called him a friend just now, I was speaking figuratively. What I am fishing for is whether Brindley seemed to you to be trying to hide anything while you were on his premises."

"Well, now you come to mention it, sir—"

"I would say he is a man who is not at his ease about something."

"I was under the impression that he was trying to hide *everything*."

It was at this moment that Wickham-Skeith came into the bar, his lungs still charged with Millicent Millicheap's home perm. When he caught sight of Mosley sharing a table with the cream of the world's espionage services, he smartly averted his eyes, ordered a double Scotch at the counter, drank it in one swallow and left.

"I am just an ageing copper, near to retirement, and with a largish rural area to try to keep in some sort of order. If you three widely experienced gentlemen could see your way to being more precise—"

"There was a woodpile in a corner," Kincaid III said, "and I happened to look at it because there were bolts and hinges in it that must have been centuries old. He almost panicked, went out of his way to draw me away from it."

"I know that stack of timber. He is under the impression that we think it may be the framework for a cock-fighting pit—a sport that is illegal in this country."

Chetverikov chipped in.

"I looked over the door of a pig-sty. When I retire, I am going to keep pigs. It will seem such a clean and friendly occupation. He was very angry in case I should disturb an ailing animal."

"He thinks that I think he has an illicit still in that sty. Of course, I have no reason to suspect anything of the kind."

Pacifico's hand wandered downwards, then he apparently remembered that he had reassured himself of his nether security only seconds ago. He laid his fingers on the table.

"His sheet-cart fascinated me. Why scrape out every last shred of sheet, when all you do is fill it up with more sheet? He does not look to me as if he has a phobia about personal hygiene."

"A phobia against personal hygiene, more likely."

Then Mosley apparently spotted someone he knew across the room, excused himself and carried his pint to another table.

Teddy Bemrose did not even pretend to be glad to see him.

Millicent Millicheap had at last succeeded in detaching the three-pin plug from her vacuum cleaner and refixing it to her hair-dryer, after much laborious scraping of rubber from the cable. By the time her door-bell rang again, she had dried out her hopeless fringe. But by no stretch of her imagination could she admit that this had brought about any improvement to appearance.

This time the caller was Mosley, who seemed wholly oblivious of the noisome atmosphere into which he walked.

Millicent Millicheap had no sort of crush on Mosley, but she was surprised at how glad she was to see him. He was

so much easier to talk to than Wickham-Skeith. There was
something rooted about Mosley. Predictable was the last
adjective one could possibly apply to him, but Mosley *belonged*.

He went straight to her table, removing his hat but not
his coat.

"Do you mind if I sit here and write a poem?"

"Of course, Mr. Mosley—but I didn't know—"

Mosley helped himself to a sheet of her notepaper and
one of her felt-tip pens and spent some minutes in absorbed
lyrical creation. When he had finished, he read through his
effort twice and seemed satisfied by it.

"Miss Millicheap, this must appear in this week's paper
over your signature."

"Oh, Mr. Mosley—"

"I know that I am asking a lot, Miss Millicheap. I know
that I am taking a treacherous liberty with your literary
reputation. But we all have to make a sacrifice sometime
or other in some noble cause."

"That was almost precisely what Mr. Wickham-Skeith
said."

"Wickham-Skeith? Has he been here?"

"You have not missed him by long. He too gave me a
poem to publish under my name."

"May I see it, please?"

There was nothing compromising about Mosley's tone of
command. She went to her bureau, where she had already
secreted Wickham-Skeith's composition.

Mosley read it, screwed it up into a ball and set fire to
it in Miss Millicheap's hearth.

"Mr. Mosley—"

"Rubbish!" Mosley said. "He has the wrong idea altogether. I don't want you to make any mistake about this,
Miss Millicheap. My poem must go to the press as it
stands. It will get things moving. Now I want your firm
promise—"

"Of course I promise. You know you can trust me, Mr.
Mosley."

"When Wickham-Skeith reads this, he'll be round here
like a shot. You must tell him that the original man from

the Warning Station has been here again and given it to you. He may get quite excited about that."

Mosley then left the house very abruptly indeed. Perhaps he was not unaware after all of the vapours that still clung. Only after he had left did she pick up his work and read it. There was a ballad-like directness about his approach that she was aware was missing from her own execution.

> If you want to know the secret,
> I know where it is,
> I know where it is,
> I know where it is,
> If you want to know the secret,
> I know where it is.
> It's driving through the sludgy night.
> And the man with all the key-words
> Is a one-eyed charioteer,
> One-eyed charioteer,
> One-eyed charioteer.
> The man with all the key-words
> Is a one-eyed charioteer,
> Driving through the sludgy night.

"Somebody's bound to suspect that that's not my work," Millicent Millicheap said to herself.

Chapter Twenty

Wilfred Weskitt crept round-shouldered into his study, but he left the door open, as he had done in the hall when he saw that Mosley had brought Cindy home. He sat down with his back to his desk and to her, looking moodily, perhaps without seeing much, out into the shrubbery where Miss Scratby and her vigilantes had had the thrill of their lives.

Cindy waited for him to speak, but it was a long time before he did. She was the one who was at fault. So unless he was prepared to prolong an impervious silence until late into the night, she wanted him to be the first to bring a new thought into the action. She did not interpret his silence as sulkiness, for the paradoxical reason that no man could have more to sulk about.

She could of course have approached him physically, highly knowledgeable as she was about the fingertip touches that had always put all things right for them until now. But she knew that there was every chance that he would repulse her. It would seem like rejecting her for cheapness, and that could be fatal, perhaps even final. And if something fortuitous were to anger her, she knew that her present contrition might dissipate like a summer morning mist.

After ten minutes of impasse, he swivelled round in his chair.

"You know, we are doing the very opposite of what we have always said we would do. We have gone to pieces because we are accused of unorthodoxy."

"I know that," she said. "But I just talked to Inspector Mosley. He made everything simple. I think he understood perfectly why we have behaved as we have since we came here—all our teaching by shocking. He also convinced me that that way is untenable in Upper Crudshaw. He convinced me simply by saying so. What's happened is my fault. I forced a capricious unorthodoxy on you."

"I didn't have to let you. So where do you want us to go from here?"

"I think we both know that, don't we? It's easier to know than to do, of course."

"Especially since an unaccommodating archdeacon has to be accommodated *en passant*."

"Bugger the archdeacon!"

"I have no difficulty in going along with that. But we can only take that attitude for the rest of today. Come the dawn—"

There was no more danger in fingertip tenderness. She went to him.

When Mosley got home it was late—too late for him to expect to see light behind his front-room curtains. It could only prognosticate yet another caller.

Susan Tunnicliffe was sitting in his favourite armchair, his wife in her own. The pair of them seemed to be getting on swimmingly.

Mrs. Mosley got up.

"I'm afraid you'll have to move, Miss Tunnicliffe. He'll go mad if he has to sit and see this room from an unfamiliar angle. Disorientation's a terrible thing."

Susan Tunnicliffe was dressed for visiting, as far as the Crudshaw portion of her wardrobe permitted: a dowdy blouse, with white bow hanging untidily down from her throat, a heather-tweed skirt that she might possibly have borrowed from her mother and a pair of crinkled leather knee-boots.

"Miss Tunnicliffe has been telling me what it was like for her, growing up in Upper Crudshaw," Mrs. Mosley said.

"I don't think that would interest your husband much. I should think he has a pretty good idea already. That isn't my problem, Mr. Mosley. I think I may safely claim to have solved that one by now. It's this marriage of my mother's—"

"It worries you?"

"Not for the first reason that might strike you, Mr. Mosley. I know the man's a crook. I know it's touch and go whether he'll go straight from now on. It's always on the

cards that the poor bugger just *can't*. I know that you lot
will have him on suspicion the moment you can. I know
that your friend Marsters will be gunning for him till they're
both on their deathbeds. But all that's beside the point. It
might even be that a short spell apart will be just what they
need to keep them perpetually sweet on each other. That's
not my main worry."

"So what is?"

"Willy Barber has already defaulted once. I don't want
that to happen again. I want him under starter's orders in
that Registry Office on time. I don't want my mother's heart
broken again. And I'll tell you an honest truth, Mr. Mosley.
I'd just as soon she was Willy Barber's responsibility as
mine for the next few years."

"There's no love lost between you?"

"It wouldn't be true to say that. We've been getting on
famously—with Willy Barber providing four-fifths of the
entertainment and nine-tenths of the therapy. But love could
easily wear a bit thin, if we saw too much of each other—
and that would be a pity. I couldn't live with her and work."

"And what do you suggest I can do about it?"

"I thought you might have a word with Willy Barber,
next time you see him."

"It's nice to know the general public believes we have
our uses," Mosley said.

"Willy Barber has told me a few stories about you, Mr.
Mosley. You don't come out of them at all badly, if I may
say so. He has a deal of respect for you, has Willy."

"So let's get on to this other subject, shall we, Miss Tunnicliffe?"

"What other subject's that, Mr. Mosley?"

"What you were talking to my wife about. Your difficulties, growing up in Crudshaw."

"I don't think that's either interesting or relevant."

"You were prattling away about it happily enough when
I came in. It interests me."

"I can't think of anything more boring. All I was telling
Mrs. Mosley was how I was put to the piano when I was
seven. *The Bluebells of Scotland*. And when I graduated
from *Underneath the lamplight's glitter* to *Where have all
the flowers gone?* they felt that I really was getting some-

where. But I wanted to do other things. I wanted to make a noise, just to annoy them. I wanted to improvise, for hours on end. I didn't know why at the time, and I'm not sure I know why now. I told them I wanted to make my own music, and I made it. I nearly drove them all mad. What I was experimenting with didn't mean a thing to them. Even a Bach Toccata had them clamouring for *My old man's a dustman.*"

She pulled a face at the boredom of forced reminiscence.

"My impromptus didn't mean much to my music teacher, either. But you don't want to hear about her."

"No, I don't, really. What I want to hear about are the other things. Growing up among your brothers, disciplined by your parents—"

"I've nothing to complain about at the end of the day, have I? I'm here. I'm what I am—in spite of anything else that might have happened."

"And it didn't always look as if it was going to come off, did it? Your father wasn't what you'd call the most flexible of men, was he?"

"He was a man without ideas—and he did his best to force lack of ideas on everyone else. But why are we talking about this, Mr. Mosley?"

"Because I want to talk about it. How would you briefly sum up your father, Miss Tunnicliffe?"

"He was mean."

"Many people would just have said careful."

"Careful? I'll say he was careful. Do you know he'd never spent a penny of his army gratuity. He wouldn't let my mother have a TV. She had a gas cooker that was a daily hazard. He would never have thought of buying a small secondhand car. He always boasted that once he'd sent us out into the world, it was no use any of us coming back to him if we got into financial difficulty. What he had banked was not enough to go round—so none of it was going anywhere. Even in old age, he wouldn't release the odd two hundred quid that would have bought him and my mother a holiday over the odds."

"You say *what he had banked.* What bank are we talking about, Miss Tunnicliffe? Where had he put his money?"

"What can it possibly matter where he had put it?"

"It matters because it didn't stay there, that's why, Miss Tunnicliffe. It was bled from him. I think you know what I'm talking about."

"I haven't the faintest idea."

"I think that you have. And if I weren't an experienced man, it would surprise me that you have come anywhere near me."

There was fire in her eyes now, and her cheeks were overheated.

"I wouldn't lose my temper if I were you, Miss Tunnicliffe. You might give too much away."

"What the hell am I supposed to make of that?"

"You couldn't stay away from me, could you? You couldn't stay away from the man who's been up to something with old Teddy Bemrose: the man who's been doing mental arithmetic with all the 2s and 2s and 2s. It isn't a new syndrome, you know. This isn't a late twentieth-century trap you've let yourself fall into. Ever since policemen have worn plain clothes, there've been a few of them hanging about at the funeral of any man who's been murdered, just to see who was standing back in the shadows because he couldn't bear to stay away."

"I wish you'd stop talking in riddles. If you've anything to say, come out into the open."

"I don't think the time's quite ripe for that yet, Miss Tunnicliffe. But I'm working on it."

A mentally retarded young man in the Saracen's Head behind Bradburn cattle market was having trouble with a home-rolled cigarette that was too tightly packed to stay alight. It was Sergeant Beamish, grinning foolishly as he cadged a match, leaning down so that he could hear the conversation of a group of farmers who were talking with relish of the misfortunes of a friend.

Wilson Ducker of Cresset Bottoms was being so hard pressed by his feed merchant that he was having to sell off a third of the flock he had at large up Cresset Bank. One of his sons had already gone up with two dogs to start bringing them down, and they would be up for auction this time next week.

Very satisfying. The tale that Nelson Brindley had put out was on its way round.

Mosley did not hurry to Michael Maguire's cell when a not unreluctant hospital released him into custody.

"Mr. Mosley—you've been taking your time, so you have. How much longer are you going to stand between a man and his bail? The bars have been open half an hour already."

"Till the man's told me a few things."

"Might I ask you to speak a little more softly, Mr. Mosley?"

Maguire's enforced jocularity was a case of making the most of a very bad job. He closed his eyes as if the effort of speech had jarred his brain beyond a man's toleration.

"I don't suppose you have a bottle of Guinness about your person, Mr. Mosely? Now wouldn't you think that the hospital authorities would know the only sort of medicine for a dying man? I asked for a bottle of porter with my breakfast, and a ward sister seven feet tall came and shouted in my ear from four inches."

Mosley put his hand into his greatcoat pocket and brought out a bottle of stout.

"Mr. Mosley—if only you knew some of the beautiful things I've been saying to people about you."

"But I haven't got a bottle-opener," Mosley said.

"Well, all you have to do is bang on the cell door and ask them to bring us one. I happen to know that the sergeant jailer keeps one on his key-chain."

"In a little while, perhaps," Mosley said.

"Now this is torture, Mr. Mosley. I'll get on to Amnesty International first thing when I'm out. What was it you were wanting to know? Quick questions will get quick answers from a man in my condition."

"About Susan Tunnicliffe—"

"Now perhaps I might ask you a question about Susan Tunnicliffe first."

"Such as?"

"Such as if it's true she's clicked on with this pasty-faced jack o'lantern from the Gestapo."

"When last seen together, they were going great guns. They have things in common that you and she never had."

Maguire closed his eyes again.

"So you ask me your question now."

"How did she pick up the cash she was thumb-screwing out of her father?"

"He had to leave it on a Thursday evening under the third pew back in Upper Crudshaw parish church."

"And what had she got on him?"

"He'd had something going with some old bag in the hills, all of fifteen years ago—and he daren't let it get to old Annie's ears. But don't be too hard on their Susan, now, Mr. Mosley. She gave every penny of it to her Mum."

Mosley brought down the bottle against a corner of the bunk, cleanly removing the crown cork. He passed the Guinness to Maguire.

"I'll never forget this, Mr. Mosley. If ever I see you drowning, I'll go off and take swimming lessons."

Chapter Twenty-one

Cindy Weskitt woke very early, unrested but decisive. The Weskitts slept in twin beds, but it had not been until the small hours that Wilfred had gone back to his. He was sleeping now with the sweetness of innocence and she was careful not to wake him. It would be soon enough when he came to and remembered the *démarches* demanded by the day ahead. It had been a bad moment for Cindy when that sour realization had come back to her a few minutes ago.

But she had things to do, and the first of them had to be done early. Upper Crudshaw was still in its slumbers as she walked into town, trying to be stealthy without appearing so. She was carrying a small tin of paint and a brush, both of which she believed must be stridently conspicuous. But a red van unloading mail-bags in the Post Office yard was the only illuminated activity.

Anyone seeing her at work must surely be tempted into making a citizen's arrest. But when a woman passed by the telephone box—a cleaning woman, on her way to one of the banks—she looked right into it, but did not do anything, say anything or even look anything. Apparently she considered it normal for the vicar's wife to be at her chores before dawn, painting out a list of the intimate services offered by an elderly solicitor's clerk.

Another character engaged in painting, though later in the day, was Nelson Brindley, who was touching up the rear doors of his night-soil wagon. It was not that the back of the vehicle needed paint—at least, not more obviously than any other part of it, but he was working with diligence and care, the unwonted artistry demanding furious concentration from his eye. He was in fact applying his single optic so single-mindedly that he was untypically unaware that strangers were mounting his hill: had, indeed, mounted it, had entered his yard, had come up on his blind flank and scared him out of his wits by addressing him.

"Your notice says you do pots of tea."

"In season," Nelson Brindley said, with all the relish of an outpost about to deny refreshment to wayfarers.

"Tea, like gorse bloom, is always in season," the wayfarer said. He was a tall and no doubt to Brindley's eye suspiciously clean man, and he was gripping a tourist's staff. He had at his side a young lady with her head wrapped in a cotton scarf.

Brindley's eye checked all corners of his yard, as if calling the roll of every angle and possession that might be interpreted as evidence of criminal activity. He then renewed his study of his visitors.

"The wife's out shopping and I've got dirty hands," he told them.

Susan Tunnicliffe resisted the temptation to point out that he could wash them: perhaps he could not stomach such an interruption to the rhythm of his day.

Brindley moved over and closed the upper half of his sty door before they could show any interest in what might be behind it. Wickham-Skeith and Susan Tunnicliffe exchanged an expressive glance.

The reality of love at first sight is often a talking point, but it is not amenable to logic. If people believe they have fallen in love at first sight, who is to say they are mistaken? The fat is usually in the fire whether they are mistaken or not. Susan Tunnicliffe did not know all that was going on in Wickham-Skeith's mind, but she had seen other men look at her in the same way. Usually they were men she would have pitied, if she had been a pitying woman—or if they had not bored her rigid.

She knew there were pros and cons. The salient quality of Wickham-Skeith (apart from his income, his presentability, his status and his transparent reliability) was that he seemed to understand her creative mind. He understood it without fawning over it, took it for granted without ignoring it. His looming drawback was that if ever there was a case of public school sexual hang-up, he must surely be one. There were things that Wickham-Skeith would need to be taught: he was probably a virgin. But this thought did not over-trouble Susan Tunnicliffe. If she could teach invertible counterpoint, she could instil a few basic configurations into Wickham-Skeith. In fact she would so train his appetites and table manners that she would be able to do anything with him that she wanted.

Two other things had entered into her objective decision to go for him. One was that she was truly weary of having to glower defiantly at the world in defence of her way of life till now. She hated herself for the thought that it was time to settle down, but there might be a bonus of fun in going one better than the college staff at their own social games. The other factor that influenced her was that she had been childish enough to become jealous of the attentions that Wickham-Skeith had been paying to Millicent Millicheap.

But last night she had had the disturbing interview with Mosley. She had been a fool to go and see him. She tried to deny to herself that there was any sense in what he had said about her being haunted by the danger that he represented. But it was true that she had felt a nasty tremor when the word went round Upper Crudshaw that he was in cahoots with that old idiot Bemrose. There was indeed something of the rabbit and snake confrontation about herself and Mosley.

She knew very little about the law, though she did know that they made a big thing of not taking kindly to blackmailers. She felt no moral responsibility for her father's suicide. It had been a shock, of course—but if that was the way he chose to react, then that was his affair. By hanging himself he had in fact solved more problems than he had created. Unless bloody Mosley was going to terrier-worry this—

She was not sure how much he would be able to prove. She could think of several reserved defences for herself, and any reasonable lawyer would surely be able to go several stages better. But she did not need to be told that long before things came to that pass, Wickham-Skeith would have sheered off: a man in his position.

So she had not been in much of a talking mood during their country walk so far. Wickham-Skeith had leaped to the clumsy conclusion that she was still resenting Millicent Millicheap. He pointed out that he had had to show an interest in the lank-haired poetess in order to investigate

her. So the additional cloud had now settled over Susan
Tunnicliffe that this might equally be true of the interest
he was taking in her.

At no point in their walk up the hill had any part of their
bodies touched. Wickham-Skeith was in better trim than
her: he must surely take more exercise than she did, for
she took virtually none. He did not moderate his pace to
walk with a woman and she did not care to show herself
either plaintive or inferior.

He had said nothing to her about the purpose of their
climb to Brindley's, beyond admitting that it had a purpose.

"Keep your eyes open while we're up there," was all he
had said. "You might just notice something that I miss."

"What are we looking for?"

"Anything noticeable."

That was how they came to look into each other's eyes
when they saw Brindley's unease about his sty. Wickham-
Skeith brought out his warrant card.

"I am a police officer on assignment from New Scotland
Yard. I wish to ask you a few questions."

Brindley scanned him with contempt for the whole of his
kind.

"You served tea and cake to three men on the afternoon
of the seventeenth of this month. Can you tell me who they
were?"

"Foreigners."

His tone implied that any abnormalities were thereby
accounted for.

"What did they want?"

"Tea."

"What did they want to know?"

"Everything."

"About what?"

"They kept on about seeing an English farm. You'd have
thought they'd never seen one before."

And would they judge the agricultural welfare of the
country by what they saw here?

"So what did you show them?"

"Nothing."

During this futile interchange, Susan had managed to
move out of Brindley's arc of vision. He was an easy man

to face with a second front. She brought herself round to the door of the sty and snatched its upper half open.

"Yuck!"

Brindley twisted away from facing Wickham-Skeith.

"I've told everybody to keep out of there. Too many noses poking in. She died on me this morning."

Wickham-Skeith did not prolong his questioning. Getting sense out of this man was work for a specialist—a specialist with time, patience—and the same wave-length as Brindley's. It was not even clear so far whether there was any sense in the man to be plumbed.

It was grey and windy, and wet under foot, but it had not actually rained since they had set out. The ground that they were treading was guide-booked as one of the most commendable hill-walks in the region, though its beauty today was mostly in cloud formations and cliff-hanging trees emerging from distant mist. Wickham-Skeith stopped now and then to lean aristocratically on his staff and look out over the vista.

"Do you know—I could envy you for living here?"

"Could you?"

"For whole half days at a time, I think. I'm essentially *homo urbis* myself."

"Well, so am I. Not *homo*, of course—" She struggled back through years to remember the Latin word. "*Mulier*. I don't live here. Couldn't. Just visiting. But it's beautiful. It seems to give me a different sense of time and self."

Whatever was disturbing her, whatever was threatening, she must subdue it for the rest of the way down this hill. It could be her last chance with Wickham-Skeith.

"Mind you, I could let the open air play a greater part in my life than it does," he told her.

"So could I," she said.

"There's something to be said for a new sense of time and self."

Then suddenly she plunged down in among the sodden grasses at the edge of the track and came up with an exquisitely tiny flower.

"Now isn't that perfection in miniature?"

She held it out in the palm of her hand, and their fingers touched as he took it from her.

"I'm sure it's something rare—in bloom to mark our passage."

"Ivy-leaved speedwell, *veronica hediflora*. Grows absolutely everywhere."

"But surely not as early as March, as a rule?"

"Through twelve months of the year. But I agree, it's beautiful, if you bother to look. That's what's missing in my life. I need stimulating to look at common speedwell and the like."

"I need stimulating, too."

Chapter Twenty-two

Beamish and Deirdre had made one of their evening outings to a hill-top inn that even by the standards of the district was remote and unfrequented—and not in the operational areas of either of them.

That afternoon, Deirdre had paid to have her hair done in a fashion currently favoured by the Princess of Wales. She knew that that lady had more promising material on which the stylist could go to work, but she was also determined to do the best with what she had. She had to derive the maximum of femininity from a frame to which she had denied it throughout her formative years. The end product was perhaps not pin-up portraiture, but it was feminine, and it was Deirdre. Beamish, in a polo-necked Aran sweater with brushed denim trousers, looked immaculately casual.

The evening was to be a memorable one for several reasons. Firstly, they talked very little vocational shop, either about social welfare or detection. They did discuss the rival merits of the Mediterranean and the Lakes, and critically studied calculations that each had made about amalgamation of available capital, about rates of mortgage interest and the advantages of endowment insurance.

Then Beamish drank a pint more than his self-disciplinary code allowed, and his mental arithmetic about milligrammes per millilitre led him to apologize in some confusion. Deirdre tut-tutted satirically.

The final unprecedented event was that when they came to the end of drinking-up time, Beamish's car refused to start. This did not suprise Deirdre, for during one of her exits from the bar she had been to remove the rotor-arm from the distributor—only to find that Beamish had already taken that step.

The landlord was a quiet observer of what was going on behind the faces of his customers, and when they asked him if he had a letting-room vacant, he assumed that they only wanted one.

Their breakfast had necessarily to be early and unleisurely. But they did speak over it about their day's work, and Deirdre asked when he would be seeing Mosley again.

"Mosley," Beamish said, "has warned me off. He wants me to have nothing to do with him."

"Surely you haven't offended him?"

"Not at all. He did something similar to me once before. It's his way of making sure I'm not caught up in the repercussions of his latest ploy."

"What is it this time?"

"I don't know. But he's sailing closer to the wind than I've ever known even him do."

"You mean with Special Branch?"

"No. With Susan Tunnicliffe. I doubt whether any case could be brought over that blackmail issue. She isn't going to confess. Old Reuben isn't going to rise out of his urn to lay a complaint, and they wouldn't convict on Maguire's evidence. But Mosley ought to tell somebody. He ought to make a report and clear the file. But he's keeping it to himself. Mosley is up to something fresh."

It was, officially, the ACC's O group, but Grimshaw did all the effective briefing. He addressed them from a blackboard map in comprehensive military fashion, with start-lines, convoy distances, flanking formations, passwords, wireless silences, lines of communication—even a base sub-area PW cage for sheep taken in the field.

But there were difficulties. Operation *Bo-Peep* was an immovable feast fixed for them by the rumour planted by Nelson Brindley. It was also the night of Operation *Final Blanket*, to be mounted by Wickham-Skeith, who had called in a company of SAS, observers from SIS and need-to-know men from most of the MIs. He had also borrowed—naturally at Chief Constable level—vast contingents from the Bradburn, the Bradcaster and neighbouring forces. Grimshaw and the ACC, who still had their standing obligations *in re* the Queen's Peace, were conscious that it was a pitifully small task force with which they were left marching as to war. Someone asked whether Mosley's talents were not to be tapped for the occasion.

"Mosley," Grimshaw said, "is far too heavily committed."

He had never known the man so busy, so ubiquitous. There followed speculation, much of it frivolous, about the pattern of Mosley's movements.

"I am reminded of a line of Stephen Leacock's," Grimshaw said. " 'He rushed off madly in all directions.' "

But he had a sad feeling that this was Mosley's swan song. After Operation *Final Blanket* had been stood down, Mosley's accounts were going to be audited.

Deirdre and Beamish were not the only ones who dined and slept away from their home territory.

By the time they reached the foot of Nelson Brindley's hillside, Susan Tunnicliffe and Wickham-Skeith had laid bare new and unexpected strata in each other. Susan had discovered that in addition to his other wide-ranging parts, Wickham-Skeith also fancied himself as a syncopated pianist in the idiom of the early twenties and that he had had a weakness in his sentimental adolescence for the novels of Gene Stratton Porter. *A Girl of the Limberlost* had been one of the three books owned by Susan's mother. Susan had read three chapters of it when she was a girl and was now able to expand them into a colourable show of expertise.

She was beginning now to toy with the idea of taking the usual steps towards advancing matters between them. The usual steps? She did not need to be told that although both the principles and the outcome remained roughly the same, a somewhat different technique was going to be needed from that which had won over more than one promising candidate from a building site. For Wickham-Skeith something more oblique was going to be needed, something less immediately suggestive of a tribal initiation on the fringes of a jungle. Only once or twice in her life—in order to relieve the boredom of ghastly and unavoidable parties— had she playfully pitted her wiles against some coy victim of protracted puberty. She had invariably failed, managing every time to drive her prey into blushing retreat. She must not take dicey chances with Wickham-Skeith. The stake was her future. But Susan Tunnicliffe was also beginning to know that she was ready for Wickham-Skeith now.

The solution to her problem came as a surprise.

* * *

The Assistant Chief Constable had drafted an *Order of the Day*, to be typed, duplicated, and his individual copy put into the hands of every soldier ear-marked for the line. St. Crispin's Day had nothing on *Bo-Peep*.

The force was going to strike a definitive blow for the security of private property. It was to be a night they would be proud of. There might be other, more gloriously sung encounters on other hillsides (a tongue-in-cheek reference to *Final Blanket*, which he thought his troops would be shrewd enough to see) but the humble sheep was the blood and lymph of their area and every man's part was vital, however unglamorous. He was relying on them all. The ACC stopped short of Montgomery's *Lord mighty in battle*, but *Bo-Peep* was to be his Alamein.

He read through the finished document, screwed it up into a ball and dropped it into his wastepaper basket. He looked at his watch. In another hour it would be time to go down to the transport yard and inspect his column formed up for the dress rehearsal.

Wickham-Skeith was silent as they turned into the last stretch before Upper Crudshaw. Susan Tunnicliffe would have put her hand over some men's fingers as they clasped the knob of the gearstick, but she was beginning to be neurotic about the dangers of scaring off Wickham-Skeith.

"I think that this afternoon deserves a celebration," he said. "What was the phrase you used? A fresh discovery of time and self? It isn't every day one makes it. What say we push the old coracle out?"

"I'm standing by with boathook at the ready."

"The only thing is, I think we ought to go a fair way from anywhere connected with impending action. Don't get me wrong. I'm not putting professional considerations first. I just think it's better to keep them well apart from our private lives."

"I think we certainly should."

"I know the ideal place, but it's forty miles from here. We'd be late back, and I hate being inhibited from an extra glass of wine. How long would it take you to pack a bag?"

A parlously short time, bearing in mind what she had with her in Crudshaw. What she needed was an afternoon in Lord Street, Southport. But there was a trend-conscious new boutique in town, surely about to go bankrupt, and she might accidentally find something worth wearing there.

"A couple of hours," she said.

"Your mother won't get the wrong idea if you stay out all night?"

The old woman was only too likely to get the right idea at the first mention of it.

"She trusts me," Susan said.

So in the early evening, with sunset a vestige of memory behind them, Wickham-Skeith drove sleekly and always on the verge of the limit, to a tastefully modernized moorland pub called the Loaders, famous for the fact that the couples who slept there were rarely man and wife.

Their breakfast the next morning was both late and leisurely. Susan was still more than slightly dazed. It was no longer a question of finding a new time and self. She felt as if both had somehow gone adrift.

At reception she had stood back while Wickham-Skeith signed the register. Only when the porter was leading them from the lift did she know for certain that it was to a double room.

At dinner Wickham-Skeith corrected several fallacies that she had always believed about wine. He quoted liberally from Browning and Causley. He revealed a fantastic, all but impossible knowledge of the few of her works that had been performed. Had he had Special Branch working on that, too?

When asked if they wanted their coffee served in the lounge, he had said that they would prefer it in their room, and shortly after that he had made the opening moves of a repertoire of erotic versatilities such as she had not met since a short-lived encounter with a Maltese clerk of works in Salford. Of course, Wickham-Skeith must have had some exotic assignments in his time. He had had to learn to live up to connoisseurs' standards. Also he had staying-power, which helped to account for her feeling of unreality over grapefruit juice and cereals.

But there was also an irritant at breakfast, in the form of a stubby little man at a neighbouring table. Even with his back to her, Susan had no difficulty in recognizing Mosley.

And how the hell had he followed them here? She came nowhere near to appreciating the extent and perspicacity of his rural intelligence service, once he had really started tapping his sources.

Her first thought was for them to escape before he could pounce on her. But Wickham-Skeith was at the very moment talking in positive terms about the joy of taking his time over bacon and eggs. So the best she could fall back on was to manipulate things so that Mosley could somehow talk to her without letting Wickham-Skeith know what it was about. Time enough for him to hear of that when she told him herself. She excused herself and got up from the table, leaving Wickham-Skeith eating heartily. Mosley also got up.

When Mosley left the Loaders, he drove to Upper Crudshaw, where his first call was at the Hanging Gate. The first of the international trio that he found was Mr. Pacifico, sitting alone in a closed and deserted bar, reading the daily newspaper produced for licensed victuallers. Mosley sat down beside him, with the *Guardian* in his hand, prominently open at the poem about sludgy night, supposedly by Millicent Millicheap.

"I have it on good authority," Mosley said, "that the one-eyed charioteer will ride tonight."

When Susan Tunnicliffe had got up from the breakfast table, she had played into Mosley's hands, for it was Wickham-Skeith, not her, that he had come to see. He waited until the Special Branch man had reached his last cup of *café au lait*, and asked permission to join him at his table. Wickham-Skeith conceded with visible displeasure.

"If I may, sir, I would like to give you a full explanation of what has been going on in Upper Crudshaw before, during, and since my absence in Spain."

And he went on, making himself sound very foolish indeed, to tell the whole story of Teddy Bemrose, Horace

Kettle, Millicent Millicheap, the Rugger Buggers and the Weskitts.

"I think you are a stupid man, Mosley. And you have gone blundering into things that you cannot begin to understand. And how you could think that such a madcap scheme could explain an old man's suicide—"

"But, sir, I am coming to that. It did lead me to the reason for the old man's suicide."

And he outlined the case, such as it was, against Susan Tunnicliffe.

"Have you reported this to your superiors?"

"No, sir. Not yet, sir. Since you are the senior officer handling this case, I thought—"

"You have shown a shred of wisdom at last, it seems. Of course no prosecution could go forward against Miss Tunnicliffe on the evidence you have adduced."

"That is what I think, sir. But I can hardly stamp *No action* on it on my own authority."

"Then use mine. Just think of the distress you would cause the Tunnicliffe family, if all this had to be opened up—and to no purpose."

"That is precisely what I am thinking, sir."

"Then let it die."

"Thank you sir. And may I ask you if you will come with me to see Archdeacon Winter?"

"Why the blazes should I want to go and see an archdeacon?"

"To help to tidy up relationships at Upper Crudshaw vicarage, sir."

"Why should it matter to me what happens to the Weskitts?"

"I do feel at some moments, sir, that my detective-superintendent ought to be told about the paper case against Miss Tunnicliffe."

"All right, blast you. When can we go and see this Venerable?"

"With your permission, I will ring the gentleman in question. There is just one more point, sir."

"No, Mosley—not another!"

"There are three aliens, temporarily resident in Upper Crudshaw—"

"Yes, yes, Mosley."

"I have heard along the grapevine that they are planning an armed attack on a night-soil cart tonight."

"Is this another of your quixotic romances, Mosley?"

"No, sir. It is from a source that has never let me down."

Chapter Twenty-three

Defined in at least one dictionary as "the bishop's eye," an archdeacon is responsible for discipline in his diocese. Archdeacon the Venerable Edmund Winter was a disciplinarian for whom black was black and white white. Yet he was a jolly man, who had no problems, not being out of tune with the majority of his clergy, who felt protected by his sleeve-worn conservatism. His only difficulties arose from the likes of Wilfred Weskitt, whose standpoint he was not mentally equipped to comprehend.

Within five minutes of seating Mosley and Wickham-Skeith in his study, Archdeacon Winter lit his pipe by striking a match against the seat of his trousers, bringing up flame from underneath himself. It was a gesture that said a very great deal about Archdeacon Winter.

Mosley let Wickham-Skeith do the talking.

"We wish to speak to you about one of your priests."

"Ah."

"The Reverend Wilfred Weskitt."

The Archdeacon settled down expecting to hear the incumbent of St. Mary's, Upper Crudshaw, accused by Special Branch of treachery to his Queen and Country, as well as against his God.

"Mr. Weskitt has been doing an undercover job for us, involving pretenses that he cannot have found palatable. He has performed with a self-control and a seam of moral courage such as have not often come my way. You will understand that I cannot go into detail, but I can assure you that without Mr. Weskitt's assistance, a current case could not have gone through to the delicate point at which it is poised."

The Archdeacon tried to strike another match. Its head broke off and fell in a second's blaze to the carpet, where he was too late to extinguish it with his foot.

"I could wish that you had informed me earlier."

"Our choice was not an easy one. We gather that—"

Wickham-Skeith smiled thinly and conspiratorially.

"We gather that Wilfred Weskitt has been thrown more than once up against your wrath."

Winter bellowed with laughter.

"That helped considerably," Wickham-Skeith said, "to convince the Queen's enemies of Weskitt's *bona fides*. In short, it enabled the deception to work. That is a prime criterion in my department."

"You must forgive me if it takes a little time for this to sink in. If I may say so, Weskitt's wife—"

"Has been the corner-stone of a tower of strength."

"Ah."

"Of course, Mr. Weskitt now wishes to restore the *status quo ante* in his parish."

"I am relieved to learn that."

"He may need your help."

"Then, by God, he shall have it!" Winter thundered.

It was generally believed that Nelson Brindley made less from farming than he did from his private enterprise disposal of what normal men find untouchable. There was a rich folklore about his nocturnal activities: he worked mostly by night. Certain imperfections in his vital vehicle made him unpopular on any premises until their residents were soundly asleep in their hermetically sealed bedrooms. Brindley was also apparently incapable of operating without contaminating himself copiously with the material of his trade. There was a story that once, in generous or absent-minded mood, he gave a lift to a benighted hitch-hiker who felt so defiled by the passenger-seat of the cab that immediately after alighting he plunged into a duck-pond. A concertina crash with Brindley's tanker was regarded as uninsurable.

Consequently when, on the night of *Final Blanket*, the silhouette of his wagon was seen climbing in the direction of Hagburn Pike, it was declared by the wits that any courting couples braving the elements would soon be beating a massed retreat upwind.

But this, like so many Nelson Brindley stories, was an idle excercise of men's imaginations. Brindley was in a strong position to fertilize a mythology, as well as fields. Although the moon was full, the skies were unromantically denuded of any shred of cloud-blanket, leaving the earth to the mercy of a cutting wind whose blades had been honed over the frozen plains of northern Europe.

Nelson Brindley gripped his steering-wheel as if he were afraid it might try to escape from him, his face held at an angle so that his eye could pierce the lunar shadows ahead.

Forward elements of Operation *Bo-Peep*, a detective-sergeant and two detective-constables from S division, were in position in Cresset Bottoms, overlooking the field in which the financially pressed Wilson Ducker was harbouring that portion of his flock that was due for Bradburn market at first light.

Grimshaw had deployed his lines according to the standard tactical practice of two up and one in reserve and the flanks were backed up by four constables in two patrol cars covering the lanes which approached Ducker's farm from either side. The reserves were in a layby up on the main road, where Grimshaw had also parked his forward HQ in a trailer caravan. The Assistant Chief Constable, reading Wilbur Smith in Bradburn station, was standing by to divert routine patrols to reinforce *Bo-Peep* at a moment's notice. Even the Chief had let it be known that he would be going to bed later than usual, and would try to keep himself awake with a book until the news had been brought to him that the campaign had been successfully concluded. One of the few members of the Bradburn force who was cosily at home that night was Mosley, who sat watching *Newsnight* with a stiff whisky and water in his hand, and his collar and tie over the arm of his chair.

Grimshaw had strictly enjoined his army that the best disguise was to look natural.

"It's unlikely that there'll be many people about, but if anyone does see you, don't draw their attention to yourself by doing anything that looks more suspicious than what you're doing already. Just look as if it's the most normal thing in the world to be doing what you're doing."

"The most normal thing in the world for me to be doing," said D-C Watkin, "is to be leaning against this sodding tree, with half an hour to go to midnight, my clothes like a dishcloth frozen on a clothes-line, gazing out into a field of sheep that I can't bloody well see."

"It's never struck me as normal that anybody should be here at all," his sergeant said. "I mean, all those prehistoric bloody hill-tribes, in the Iron Age and that—there weren't all that many people on this island in those days. So why did they want to come and settle up here? Nothing grows but grass. It hardly ever stops raining except to bloody snow. Why didn't they migrate somewhere like Bridlington, where they would at least have had the advantage of a few fish and chip shops?"

Grimshaw had decreed that there was to be no use of wireless at any stage, since he had a theory that the rustlers must have been listening in on the police net on their previous raids. Sergeant Beamish was therefore detailed as his runner, liaising with all groups and gingering them up wherever applicable.

He had just left Grimshaw for one of his circular tours when he was overtaken by a night-soil tanker being driven very fast along the Bradburn-Cowburn road. A few seconds later, it was followed by another, careering after it at reckless speed. He noticed that its tail-board bore the proclamation *Left-Hand Drive*.

Two night-soil carts? One of the most inflexible exhortations at the *Bo-Peep* final briefing was that no one was to pay any attention to any manifestation that looked as if it might be emanating from *Final Blanket*. Never the twain were to acknowledge each other.

Beamish was aware of more headlights coming up behind him, their beams inconsiderately full on, flooding his car with light, which blinded him from his mirrors and made it virtually impossible to drive. He took his foot off the accelerator, but the vehicle did not seem to want to pass him. He changed down cautiously to bottom gear, expecting to be bumped in the rear, pulled over close in on his near side at less than ten miles an hour. At last the lights began to overtake him. It was another sewage-disposal tanker, a man leaning out from the passenger-seat of the cab and shouting unintelligible abuse at him. Beamish could have sworn that it was Pete Pollitt, the crippled, non-playing secretary of the Rugger Buggers.

And immediately behind this tanker came another. Four, now. And somewhere along the road ahead of him he heard the sickening, tearing crash of metal into metal. A collision between two of those things, and this road was going to be closed to traffic until well into the hours of tomorrow's daylight.

On the diminutive village green of Comberley one of the few normal patrols still policing the hills were drinking coffee from a flask when they saw a convoy come up fast from Hassler's Clough and disappear equally hurriedly in the Cowburn direction.

"Do you think we ought to log that?" one of the constables asked the other. "Seven shit-carts in a row?"

"Probably just another of these EEC surpluses."

Beamish went up into third, trying to make sense of the wild interplay of lights stabbing up into the sky about a mile in front of him. There was no comprehensible pattern about it — and now the crashing of metal was incessant, like some monstrous, arrhythmical oil-drum band.

Beamish came cautiously over the brow of the hill and saw below him a layby formed by a loop of discontinued road, and now used by the Highways Department as a dump for tons of grit. In this layby a battle was going on between a number of tankers, butting, charging and nudging each other with total disregard for life, limb or property.

Beamish lowered his window and watched. His instructions were adamant: he was not to interfere in *Final Blanket*, even if he came upon a pitched battle. And a pitched battle this certainly was, though he was unable to see the line-up or intention of it. In so far as they stood still long enough to be counted, he made out five wagons, but it was impossible to work out who was on whose side. As far as he could see, everybody's enemy was everybody else.

Nelson Brindley collected his night's load, did a three-point turn with exaggerated stealth at a farm-track crossroads and began his juddering descent from Hagburn Brow to the comparatively main road at the bottom. He was just edging out into this road when the bonnet of some ungainly vehicle inched out from the shadows across his bows. Brindley cursed—then saw to his surprise that it was another night-soil wagon. A man jumped down from its cab and come towards him carrying a hand-torch. Brindley saw that it was Wickham-Skeith.

Wickham-Skeith had had a bad night. The SAS had been intended as his mainstay, but although their company was stationed less than thirty miles away, it had been decided to deliver them by airdrop, since no opportunity for training must be missed. They had landed in two sticks well outside their target area, and it was likely to be some three hours now before they were available where they were wanted. Then something had gone wrong with his communications with the contingents he had borrowed from local forces, and he did not know where they had got to. All he knew was that Brindley had gone up Hagburn Brow, and that Kincaid III, Chetverikov and Pacifico would be on the move by now. His department had received a full assessment of these gentlemen's intentions through the combined efforts of MI6 and SIS.

The truce between the trio had of course come to an end the moment it was clear that the action was about to begin. It had all happened before, at case-work stages when they were without information. The interminable game of Lofoten Skat had filled in the idle hours while they jockeyed with each other over what meagre gen they had picked up. But once the key-target was identified as Nelson Brindley's wagon, it was every man for himself again. Each had to acquire a wagon of his own which he could substitute for Brindley's at some critical point.

Kincaid III's, a model with Left-Hand Drive, was shipped to him by air-freight from Pittsburgh, covered in tarpaulin sheets and with the status of a diplomatic bag. Chetverikov's embassy bought him one on the open market, and Senor Pacifico acquired one through an entrepreneur who had it hi-jacked from a GLC yard in Tower Hamlets.

It followed that Wickham-Skeith had to have one too. His original plan had been to direct its operation from a well improvised map-room, but he was an adaptable man, and when he saw that he was on his own, he saw what one man had to do. That was how he came to be waiting at the foot of Hagburn for Nelson Brindley to come down.

But it was a bad error to have got out of his cab to confront Brindley. Brindley saw that he had been left with a risky inch in which to manoeuvre himself past the edge of a roadside ditch, and he managed to pull into the road just as Wickham-Skeith was approaching his cab door. Wickham-Skeith lost valuable time in getting started up to follow him. The two of them were the first to overtake Beamish at high speed.

Close behind were Kincaid III, Pacifico and Chetverikov. Behind them were two unaccountables. One was a genuine night-soil operative from Bradburn Corporation's Public Health Department, trying to be about his lawful business. The others were the Rugger Buggers, who had hired their vehicle from a scrap-yard. No one ever discovered how they knew that there was going to be a night's fun to be had: Mosley was suspected of informing them, but nothing was ever proved.

As they approached the grit-dump, Pacifico was neck and neck alongside Kincaid III and tried to force him into it. For a perilous few seconds they blocked the highway. Those behind them had no alternative but to turn into the layby. That was how battle came to be pitched.

But Brindley, with Wickham-Skeith chasing him, had gone on. Wickham-Skeith finally caught him in the deserted market square of Cowburn. Brindley had finally run out of petrol, it being one of his principles never to have too much in his tank in case his vehicle was stolen.

"Brindley, I have reason to believe—"

Wickham-Skeith did not think of it as brave, but opening the rear doors of a night-soil cart on a duty run was an act of courage at which some hardened operators would have quailed.

Not so Wickham-Skeith. He undid the retaining bolts—not without difficulty and damage to his wrist. It was remarkably clean inside the tank, though redolent of an odour that Chief Inspector Marsters would have recognized at once. Eight sheep jumped out past him into the night.

* * *

"So Special Branch have their uses after all, Tom," the ACC said.

"Yes. I think we can consider this file cleared."

"Nelson Brindley all the time—with the perfect cover-story. Wickham-Skeith ought to get a commendation."

"On the contrary, the arrest is down to Beamish, who got to Cowburn just behind them. Wickham-Skeith is anxious not to have his name mentioned in connection with the incident. The whole thing has the air of a cover-up— on the very highest authority. Except for the offences that Brindley has asked to be taken into consideration, none of this has happened. In the interests of national security."

"So what are we going to do with Mosley?"

"Return him to his normal rounds. As a matter of fact, I believe he's already out on them."

Three consecutive weddings were carried out with civic dignity. The Superintendent-Registrar was a little puzzled by the attendance. For Willy Barber, Annie Tunnicliffe, Wickham-Skeith and Susan, it was more or less a case of *places change*, except that Wickham-Skeith was Willy Barber's best man. The ACC, Detective-Superintendent Grimshaw and the Chief himself were there to support Wickham-Skeith, but only the ACC and Grimshaw stayed for Beamish and Deirdre. Mosley was the only one who attended all three ceremonies.

NERO WOLFE STEPS OUT

Every Wolfe Watcher knows that the world's largest detective wouldn't dream of leaving the brownstone on 35th street, with Fritz's three star meals, his beloved orchids and the only chair that actually suits him. But when an ultra-conservative college professor winds up dead and Archie winds up in jail, Wolfe is forced to brave the wilds of upstate New York to find a murderer.

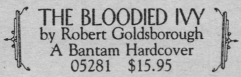

THE BLOODIED IVY
by Robert Goldsborough
A Bantam Hardcover
05281 $15.95

BANTAM
SHOP-AT-HOME
C·A·T·A·L·O·G

Special Offer
Buy a Bantam Book
for only 50¢.

Now you can have Bantam's catalog filled with hundreds of titles plus take advantage of our unique and exciting bonus book offer. A special offer which gives you the opportunity to purchase a Bantam book for only 50¢. Here's how!

By ordering any five books at the regular price per order, you can also choose any other single book listed (up to a $5.95 value) for just 50¢. Some restrictions do apply, but for further details why not send for Bantam's catalog of titles today!

Just send us your name and address and we will send you a catalog!